TREE
HOUSE
ISLAND

by

SCOTT CORBETT

Illustrated by GORDON HANSEN

AN ATLANTIC MONTHLY PRESS BOOK

LITTLE, BROWN & COMPANY
Boston • Toronto

ATLANTIC—LITTLE, BROWN BOOKS
ARE PUBLISHED BY
LITTLE, BROWN AND COMPANY
IN ASSOCIATION WITH
THE ATLANTIC MONTHLY PRESS

Published simultaneously in Canada
by Little, Brown & Company (Canada) Limited

PRINTED IN THE UNITED STATES OF AMERICA

To Mildred Morton

TREE HOUSE ISLAND

1

SKIP AND HARVEY had the *Fifteen* pulled up on the beach and were scrubbing her floorboards when the smiling fat man and the small dark-faced man appeared on the wharf above them.

For a moment the men stood looking out over the harbor. The only boats moored in it were a few pleasure craft. All the fishing boats and lobster boats had put to sea to make the most of a fair day and calm seas.

The fat man nodded his head several times.

"Splendid view, splendid. One of the most picturesque little harbors on the New England coast," he said. He pointed a sausage-shaped finger seaward. "Those are the islands, out there."

The small man neither spoke nor changed expression, but only nodded. Judging from his olive complexion, he was a Mexican, or South American. The boys had never seen either of the men before, but now that the vacation season was starting, strangers were no novelty in Goose Harbor. People were already beginning to visit the little seaside village now, looking for cottages to rent for the summer.

The fat man turned and smiled down at them.

3

"Good morning, lads!" he called in a hearty way. "And which of you is the skipper of the *Fifteen*?"

"I am, sir," answered Skip.

"I see. Well, now, is the *Fifteen* for hire?"

"Yes, sir. Fishing's not much good yet, though."

The fat man turned and nudged his friend jovially. "Now there's an honest lad, Professor. I like that." He turned back to Skip. "Fortunately, we didn't have fishing in mind, but only a little sightseeing trip. Could you run us out to those islands and back?"

"Sure."

"And what would your fee be?"

Skip considered. The two small islands lay slightly to the south of Goose Harbor. The near island was about fifteen hundred yards offshore, measuring from the Point, a promontory which lay south of the harbor. The larger island was five hundred yards farther out, east-northeast from the smaller. From the harbor to the Point was another fifteen hundred yards; thus, a round trip would be nearly four miles.

"Well, just for sightseeing, two dollars," he decided.

"Fair enough," nodded the fat man. "Can we go now?"

"Yes, sir. We'll pick you up on the float."

The boys went briskly to work replacing the floorboards, hooking back rests onto the center thwart, and putting two cushions on it. Glancing up as the fat man turned away to cross the wharf, Skip considered the impressive width of the seat of his pants.

"Maybe we'd better let him have the whole thwart to himself, and have the other man ride forward," Skip murmured.

4

Harvey's big eyes twinkled behind their thick black-rimmed glasses while the rest of his face remained perfectly straight.

"Okay, Skip," he said, and changed the seats.

They ran the big dory down into the water and swung aboard. Skip started the outboard motor and laid the *Fifteen* alongside the float in one clean sweep.

The fat man climbed down the ladder onto the float with surprising nimbleness. His small feet moved quickly and surely, so that he seemed to come down as lightly as a balloon. When he reached the float, however, the square wooden platform bobbed noticeably under the impact of his weight. He was still smiling, displaying a set of large, regular, and very white false teeth.

Behind him the dark man dropped down swiftly. Skip noticed the way he skimmed down the ladder, with the monkey-like ease of a seaman.

"Ah-ha!" The fat man laughed heartily as his small eyes took in the seating arrangements. "I see you're going to trim the boat properly, with me in the center where I can't sink her."

He laughed some more as he watched the boys' faces redden.

"Never mind, lads, you're quite right. But do switch those back rests around." They had placed them so that the passengers would be facing forward. "I want to ask you some questions along the way."

Harvey changed the back rests around so that the men could ride facing aft. The two strangers stepped into the boat and settled themselves in a way that showed an easy familiar-

5

ity with small boats. Both boys sat in the stern. Skip swung the *Fifteen* slowly away from the wharf and moved out into the channel.

The fat man was wearing a light suit and a wide-brimmed light gray felt hat. He took off his hat now and sat back enjoying the breeze that was rippling the harbor waters. He was shiny bald, and he had a deeper tan than most people have that early in the summer.

"Ah-h! This is nice — eh, Professor?" he said, calling to his friend over his shoulder. The dark man nodded, without showing any signs of enjoyment.

"Well, now, tell me," said the fat man, turning back to Skip and smiling again. "And why did you name your boat the *Fifteen?*"

"Well, I just got her this year, and fifteen seemed to be my number," said Skip. "She's fifteen feet long at the water line, and I'm fifteen years old."

"Good enough! Next you ought to get a fifteen-horse motor."

"Afraid not. I'm lucky to have a secondhand ten."

"And a nice motor it is, too. Makes very little noise, for an outboard. And what's your name?"

"Skip Ellis."

"Skip?"

"That's a nickname. Short for Skipper. That's because I've always had a boat of some kind ever since I was five years old."

"Do you live here all year, or just come summers?"

"No, I live here."

"And what about you, lad?" The fat man turned his small, keen eyes toward Harvey. "What's your name?"

"Harvey Harding, sir."

The fat man called over his shoulder again to his friend. "Polite. I like that," he said, and smiled at Harvey. "And do you live here, too?"

"Yes, sir."

"And how old are you?"

"I'm also fifteen, sir."

"Oh? Well, well."

Skip knew what the fat man was thinking. He was thinking that the owl-eyed boy, with his narrow shoulders, his thin legs, and general small size, did not look that old. On the other hand, Harvey's solemn face and his big black-rimmed glasses sometimes made him look very old.

Harvey was a boy it was easy to underrate, if you didn't know him. Among the boys who spent their summers on the waterfront at Goose Harbor, he was often spoken of by such nicknames as the Brain, and Genius — and the nicknames were half serious.

As the boat moved through the harbor mouth and Skip increased her speed, the fat man sat back and closed his eyes, a picture of enjoyment. Up forward the dark man sat twisted sideways, hunched up, expressionless, looking over his shoulder at the islands ahead. Skip glanced at Harvey, and saw that he was studying the fat man with close attention.

Oh-oh, thought Skip, *here we go again.*

If there was one fault Harvey Harding had, it was an over-

active imagination. Everything he saw suggested a story to him, usually a wild one. Every summer since he was ten he had written and directed and acted in blood-and-thunder plays and talked his friends into taking parts in them. If he had confined his storytelling to plays it might have been all right, but Harvey made up stories all the time. Small wonder, then, that Skip began to worry when he saw the way Harvey was studying their passengers. What kind of story was he building around the two strangers?

Skip dug a thumb into Harvey's lean ribs.

"All right, Shakespeare," he muttered. "Take it easy."

Instantly the fat man's eyes opened and he was smiling.

"Shakespeare?" he said. "And what has friend Harvey done to deserve such an illustrious name?"

Skip was embarrassed, but there was nothing to do but explain.

"Oh, he writes plays all the time, and he's always thinking

8

up wild stories about everything. Last week we found an old spar that had washed up on the Point — that's the Point there ahead, on the south side of the harbor entrance. Well, Harvey started making up a story about it. He pretended it was a spar from a British merchantman that had been wrecked two hundred years ago carrying gold to the colonies. It had just been uncovered after all those years, he said, and the rest of the ship must be close by, buried in the sandbank, and probably if we started raking around in the sand we'd find it was full of pieces of eight."

"Delightful idea," said the fat man.

"Yes, but a couple of new kids who didn't know Harvey came along just in time to hear the part about the pieces of eight in the sand. By then he was really throwing himself into his story. He made it sound so believable that they slipped away and ran home to get rakes. On their way they told a few people what they were up to, and that was the start of it. First thing you knew, half the town was hurrying to the Point with rakes to see if there could be any truth in the story that was flying around."

The fat man's laughter boomed out across the water. Harvey grinned sheepishly, but said nothing. As far as Goose Harbor's adult population was concerned, Harvey Harding was on probation for the moment.

"Folks felt pretty foolish when they heard the truth, of course," Skip went on, "and at first they were pretty sore at Harvey. But my father — he's the minister here — my father told them Harvey hadn't meant any harm and hadn't meant to start a rumor. He promised to have a talk with Harvey and

9

his aunt and uncle to make sure it wouldn't happen again."

Although he continued to laugh, the fat man sat forward with his hands on his knees and his small eyes were sharp while he studied Harvey as attentively as Harvey had been studying him.

"Well, well, so that's it," he said. "In that case, I'd better introduce myself and my colleague, and explain why we're interested in the islands, so that he won't make up any wild stories about us. I'm Dr. Conrad Dillingham, and this is Professor Santos of the University of Santiago. We're ornithologists, and I'm sure you boys know what that is."

"You study birds," nodded Skip. "Harvey's a bird expert himself."

"Oh?" Again Dr. Dillingham's eyes studied Harvey. "Well, that's good to hear. You'll be interested in our work, then. We're working on a project for a scientific foundation. It has to do with making a survey of the kinds of birds that frequent the islands off our Atlantic coast. So we may possibly want to spend some time on your islands. I understand a Mr. Ben Doane owns them. We stopped by his house, but he wasn't home."

"He's out lobstering," said Skip.

"So I was told. I understand there's a camp on the larger island which he sometimes rents?"

"That's right — when he can. Not many people ever want to stay out there, for fear of being cut off from the mainland by a storm."

"I can understand that."

"Do you want to go ashore there?"

10

"Yes, I'd like to. What's the island called, by the way?"

"Doane Island. It's been in Ben Doane's family for generations."

"I see. And the smaller one?"

"Well, it's been called by lots of names. It's been called Near Island, because it's closer to shore, and Speck Island, because it's so small. We kids have always called it Tree House Island, though."

"I see. And I suppose that's because you've built a tree house out there?"

"Yes, sir. We built one years ago. The little kids still use it. The hurricane of '38 knocked down all the big trees there except one. Ben Doane let us build a tree house in that one."

Doane Island lay dead ahead now. Since Skip had planned to make a circle of the islands, they were approaching the larger one first.

Doane Island was long and narrow. It would just about have held two football fields, set end to end. It pointed straight at Tree House Island, five hundred yards away.

On the narrow end nearest Tree House Island was a small clearing with a rough three-room cabin in the middle of it. The rest of the island was heavily wooded, though most of the trees were small, scrubby things. The big hurricane twenty years ago had played havoc with Doane Island, too.

On the shore in front of the cabin, a small, weather-beaten dock displayed an impressive collection of barnacles on its pilings. The tide was low, so that the planking of the dock was several feet above them as Skip brought the *Fifteen* alongside the old wooden ladder.

11

"Be careful on that ladder. It's old, and some of its rungs may be rotten," said Skip diplomatically. But Dr. Dillingham did not seem to be sensitive about his weight.

"Rotten or not, I guess the old hippopotamus had better watch his step, at any rate," he said cheerfully. "Professor, you'd better go first and throw me a line, just in case. Don't I see an extra line faked down up forward there, lads?"

"Yes, sir. You can use that," said Skip.

Professor Santos scampered up the ladder and made one end of the half-inch Manila line fast to a pile on the far side of the dock. Dr. Dillingham then went cautiously up the ladder like a mountain climber, holding tightly to the line. The boys held their breath — and the ladder held the doctor.

They made the boat fast and followed.

"Well, well. So this is Doane Island," said the doctor, leading the way off the dock with a surprisingly energetic step. "Never mind the cabin for now — we'll look at it after we've seen whether the island itself seems to hold any promise of bird life."

"Oh, there's lots of birds out here," said Skip.

"You've been here often, I suppose."

"Yes, sir."

They made a tour of the island, with Dr. Dillingham spotting birds and uttering scientific names almost every step of the way. There were nesting birds of several species.

Professor Santos scarcely spoke. The few times he did say anything in reply to the doctor's constant flow of talk, he spoke briefly in broken English.

12

"Well, I must say I think this would be worthy of a week's effort," said the doctor when they had returned to the tip of the island. "I'm sure the Foundation will agree, once we've reported, aren't you, Professor?"

The professor nodded.

"Of course, if the smaller island offers additional possibilities, it will help." He tried the door of the cabin and, finding it locked, went to a window to peer inside. "H'm. Grim prospect for living quarters, but I suppose we could manage. Well, let's shove off and have a look at the other island."

They returned to the boat and headed for Tree House Island. It was shaped like a kidney bean, with a tiny cove on the side toward shore and away from Doane Island. It was only half as long as Doane Island, and even narrower. Near the center of the island its one surviving oak rose to a height of about forty feet, surrounded by small pines and scrub oak. Even in this survivor, only a spark of life lingered, as shown by the few clusters of leaves its lower branches had put forth. The tree house in its bare upper branches stood out sharply against the bright blue sky.

"If you want to go ashore here, I'm afraid you'll have to wade," said Skip. "There's no dock."

"Anything for science," sighed Dr. Dillingham, and began to roll up his trouser legs. He removed his shoes and socks, and when the *Fifteen* grated on the sand of the tiny beach he stepped nimbly out of the boat into the shallow water, as did the professor, and helped beach the boat. With his powerful help the job was easy.

13

"Well, now, this one is really small," he commented. "Still, I suppose we might find something here just the same — eh, Professor?"

Surprisingly, the professor almost smiled. Sourly, to be sure, but still it was almost a smile.

"I hear plenty birds here," he replied as they walked up the beach to make a tour of the island. The doctor walked straight toward the center of the island, then suddenly stopped and stared around him.

"My word! That hurricane certainly did a job here, eh? Only one big tree left. And think of it — that's about twenty years ago now." He seemed to be dreaming for a moment, but then he stirred himself and glanced at his companion. "Well, Professor, I think we've seen enough, don't you? And I don't want to keep these young gentlemen out too long or the price is liable to go up for our trip," he added, smiling broadly.

"Oh, that's all right, Dr. Dillingham —" began Skip.

The fat man laid a huge arm on his shoulders.

"I was just fooling, lad. And call me Doc. I'm not a real doctor, anyway — not an M.D., that is, but only a Ph.D. A doctor of philosophy. But you know, when you're in any scientific field you have to give yourself all the impressive titles you can."

He laughed heartily and led the way back to the boat.

"Your Ph.D. is in natural history, I expect," said Harvey. It was almost the first time he had spoken, except in answer to questions. Dr. Dillingham stopped and turned to face him. His small eyes became even smaller as they narrowed slightly.

"That's quite right. In natural history." He turned to the

14

professor. "He's a smart lad, this one. I like that. Well, let's head for the harbor."

When they reached the harbor, Doc pulled out his wallet.

"Couldn't have asked for a nicer trip. Here's your money," he said, handing two dollars to Skip, "and here's something for the mate," he said, holding out a dollar to Harvey.

Harvey's long face colored.

"Oh, that's not necessary, sir."

The fat man stuffed the dollar bill down the neck of Harvey's tee shirt.

"Take it. I'm glad to do it. You mustn't insult me by refusing, because I expect the Professor and I will be around for a week or so. If we can't rent a suitable boat we may have to do further business."

"Well . . . thank you, sir."

"Just call me Doc."

"Yes, sir," said Harvey awkwardly. Dr. Dillingham stared at him for an instant. The fat man might have been a bit exasperated, or he might have been merely amused. It was hard to tell what lay behind the doctor's constant smile.

"Say, you're a bit hard to get to know, aren't you, lad? Well, never mind — we'll get better acquainted later on. See you later, lads, and thanks for everything," he said, as they came alongside the float.

"Thank you, Doc. Good-by, Professor," said Skip. The professor nodded.

"Good-by, Professor. Good-by . . . er . . . Doc, and thank you," said Harvey.

"That's better," said Doc, smiling, and made his way up

15

the ladder, with the professor following him as monkey-like as ever.

When they had gone, Skip turned to stare at Harvey. He made no bones about it, he was more exasperated than amused.

"Harvey, what was the idea of acting so funny? If he wanted to give you a buck, why should you mind?"

"I wouldn't, ordinarily," said Harvey, "but ... well ..."

"Well what?"

Harvey had an odd expression on his face. He looked embarrassed, but he also looked stubborn. He stared down at the bottom of the boat for a moment, frowning in his squinty way, and then lifted his head. The eyes behind his huge black-rimmed glasses were filled with a strange glitter.

"Well, if I don't believe his story I shouldn't take his money — and I don't believe his story," said Harvey.

2

Skip was not only exasperated, he was concerned. He didn't want to see his friend get into any more trouble. For one thing, Harvey could not afford to. There was the scholarship to think of. The scholarship, and Ephraim Fairchild.

"Now, listen, Harv," he said, as they beached the *Fifteen* again, "don't start dreaming up some wild story about Dr. Dillingham and Professor Santos."

"I'm not."

"Remember what happened about the pieces of eight. Remember how sore Eph Fairchild was about getting sucked in on it himself. You're lucky you didn't lose out on the Bayliss Scholarship altogether."

Old Ephraim Fairchild was not only the president of the local bank, he was also a trustee of the Bayliss Scholarship Fund. On the day the rumor started, he had appeared at the Point himself behind the wheel of the old green jeep he used for a beach buggy. He claimed he drove out just to see how many darn fools would fall for the story, but there were some people who swore afterwards that they saw a rake handle sticking out of the back of his jeep. This made the old gentleman

17

angrier than ever, and for a while he had declared he would see to it that Harvey Harding never received a Bayliss Scholarship.

This would have been a terrible blow to Harvey's future, because a Bayliss Scholarship would give him about his only chance to attend college. Harvey had been an orphan for nearly five years. His only relatives were an aunt and uncle who lived in Boston, and his Uncle Nate and Aunt Sarah, with whom he lived in Goose Harbor. In the winter Uncle Nate drove a school bus and worked in a lumberyard. In the summer he and Aunt Sarah ran a small inn. During the height of the season Harvey worked long hours there and more than earned his keep.

Neither of Harvey's uncles would be able to give him much help toward his college expenses, and Harvey wanted very much to go to college. The scholarship was his best hope, so it was important for him to stay out of trouble — and he had two more years to go at high school before he would be ready for college.

"Whatever crazy ideas you've got about those men, forget them," advised Skip. "Don't start cooking up some cock-and-bull story about them the way you did about that spar."

"I never claimed that story was true, did I? I'm talking about something entirely different now," said Harvey, with that stubborn look still on his long face. "I'm saying I don't think those men are what they claim to be. And I'm not making up any story about them, because I have no idea what they're up to — yet."

"No, but you're thinking up all kinds of nutty possibili-

18

ties," accused Skip. "Well, if you must suspect them of funny business, go ahead, but please — don't say anything about it to anyone but me."

"I won't," promised Harvey, and then spoiled the promise by adding, "at least, not for the present."

Skip sat down on the bow of the *Fifteen* and folded his arms.

"All right, wise guy, let's hear it. Just what is it about Dr. Dillingham and Professor Santos that makes you so suspicious? Go ahead, tell me that."

"All right." Harvey planted himself in the sand in front of Skip, his thin legs wide apart, his hands on his hips, much like a prosecuting attorney in front of a jury. "In the first place, Doc was smiling all the time, but if you ask me his eyes

19

weren't doing any of the smiling at all. They were about as soft and kind as a bluefish's."

"Well . . ." Skip remembered noticing how sharp and hard the fat man's small eyes could be, but he didn't want to admit it, since that would only encourage Harvey. "Just because he doesn't have kind and smiling eyes doesn't mean he couldn't be a scientist studying birds. Not all scientists are such swell guys personally, in fact I guess some of them are pretty cold-blooded. Say, wait a minute!" A terrible thought struck Skip. "You're not building up one of those Mad Scientist plots in your mind, like that movie we saw last week?" he asked anxiously. That would be exactly Harvey's speed! "I can just hear you, making up some crazy story about Dr. Dillingham and Professor Santos out there on their lonely island, creating a Bird Monster . . ."

But Harvey shook his head.

"No, nothing like that."

"Maybe you don't think he's a real ornithologist. I suppose you're going to tell me that all that stuff he said about the birds out on Doane Island was wrong?"

"No, you know those birds as well as I do, Skip, and you know he named them all correctly."

"How about those scientific names he rattled off in Latin?"

"They were correct, too. No, he knows something about birds, all right. But there were other things. I can't even put my finger on them, but . . . I'm sure you must have noticed one funny thing, though."

"What's that?"

20

"Professor Santos must have been a seaman at some time or other."

"Well, what of it?"

"Nothing, except that somehow you don't expect that of a professor. For that matter, they both knew how to act around a small boat."

"Yes, but that doesn't necessarily prove anything is phony about their story."

"I know. Mainly, with me, it's just a feeling . . ."

"It's your wild imagination!"

"Well, anyway, I'm certainly going to keep my eyes open if they turn up here again."

"Personally, I hope they don't, Harv. I can see you asking for trouble if they do. Don't forget that Eph Fairchild is also president of the Birdbrains," Skip reminded him. The "Birdbrains" was the local nickname for the Goose Harbor Bird Study Club, an old-established organization of bird lovers. "He'll probably roll out the red carpet for a couple of visiting ornithologists like Dr. Dillingham and Professor Santos, and he certainly won't be happy with you if you give them any trouble."

"I know, I know," said Harvey in his absent-minded way. He glanced at his watch. "Well, I've got to get back to the inn and do some chores for Aunt Sarah."

"Okay — but remember, don't say a word about Doc and the professor to anybody, not even your aunt or uncle."

"Don't worry." Harvey's thin face broadened with one of his quick grins. "But I still say —"

21

"Beat it, will you?"

Harvey scampered away still grinning as Skip picked up a piece of driftwood and threatened to clobber him with it. Skip watched him go, shook his head, and turned back to the *Fifteen*. The tide was dead low now. He ran the *Fifteen* out to her mooring and made her fast, giving her enough slack to allow her to rise with the tide, then rowed ashore in the old pram he kept at his mooring to get back and forth in. When he had beached the pram and secured her, he climbed up onto the wharf and headed for home.

The sun, low in the sky now, stretched Skip's shadow far back along the oily planks as he walked up the wharf. Some gulls sitting on the edge of the wharf took off and wheeled over the quiet water as he passed. A lobster boat puttered around the Point into the harbor. Skip turned to look. It was Ben Doane coming in. Skip wondered what old Ben would say when he heard a couple of men had been around asking about renting the islands. Maybe after supper he and Harvey ought to get together and go tell Ben about taking them out there. If Harvey would promise not to say anything about his crazy suspicions, that is.

"Hi, Skip."

From the open window of the tiny studio above his art supplies and picture-framing shop, Lee Rand waved a brush at him. Lee was a young artist. During the summer season he ran his shop, framed pictures, drew quick charcoal portraits and caricatures of tourists and summer visitors, and made enough money that way to roam around painting what he wanted to paint the rest of the year. Being located in the cor-

22

ner building at the head of the wharf, he had a choice spot to live in. Some solid citizens like Ephraim Fairchild didn't approve of Lee — he got too much fun out of life — but everybody else enjoyed having him around, especially Ephraim Fairchild's granddaughter Mary. The old gentleman did everything he could to discourage her from spending her time with Lee.

"Hi, Lee." Skip stopped under his window. "When did you get back?"

"Late last night."

"How was the graduation?"

"Very nice. Of course, I spoiled it a little for Grandpa by being there," said Lee, grinning. Mary had graduated from college the day before.

"When's she coming down?"

"She's already here. In fact, I'm hoping she'll be along any minute to take a walk on the beach."

"Oh. Then I'd better get lost."

"No, hold on. I want to know about the *Fifteen*. How do you like her?"

"Fine. She handles nicely. I made my first money with her today. Two men paid me a couple of bucks for a run out around the islands. Gave Harvey a buck, too."

"Well, good!"

"When are you going to put your boat in the water?"

"I'll slap the final coat of that new anti-fouling paint on her bottom tomorrow, and then in she goes."

"Seems a shame to waste good paint on that little old scow," said Skip, grinning up at his friend.

24

Lee took his pipe out of his mouth and pointed the stem of it down at Skip.

"Don't get fresh with the pride of the fleet, sonny. She may be small, but she's a trim craft. Just because some tycoons can go racing around in a big dory with a ten-horse motor —"

"I'd better make good money with her taking tourists out fishing, or I'll wish I'd kept the *Sea Horse*," said Skip, referring to his former, smaller boat.

For a moment he was tempted to tell Lee more about the two strangers and the worrisome way Harvey was acting, but then he decided not to say anything to anybody concerning the matter for the present. After all, maybe the whole thing would blow over. Maybe Doc Dillingham would never show his smiling face in Goose Harbor again.

While he was thinking about this, another kind of smiling face appeared around the corner. This one was the prettiest face Goose Harbor was likely to see all summer.

Mary Fairchild was small and was blessed with supple grace and high spirits. A few years back people had called her the worst tomboy Goose Harbor had ever known. She was the best swimmer and sailor of any girl around.

"Hi, Skip!" She waved, and her brown eyes twinkled as she came toward him with her hand out. "When do I get my ride in the *Fifteen?*"

"Any time, Mary," said Skip, as they shook hands. "Wish I didn't have to go home to supper, I'd take you out right now."

"Well, I'm looking forward to it. By the way, Skip, have

25

you seen a homely artist around here anywhere?" she asked, being careful not to glance up.

"Hey, Skip, who's your funny-looking friend?" asked Lee from his window.

"You know, my grandfather doesn't approve of crazy artists," Mary went on, ignoring him, "so I have to avoid them and go walking on the beach alone. I'll see you later, Skip — I guess I might as well get started."

"You know, Skip, it's a nice evening. I think I'll take a walk myself," said Lee, and disappeared from his window to come downstairs.

"Congratulations on your graduation, Mary," said Skip.

"Thank you," she said, and vaulted lightly over the wharf rail onto the beach.

"See you later, Skip," said Lee, as he hurried out of his shop and vaulted the rail to join her. Skip grinned as he watched them go arm in arm off down the beach along the water's edge. Mary was a Fairchild herself, and had a mind of her own. If her grandfather wanted to keep her from seeing Lee, he had his work cut out for him.

At home, while he was washing up in the kitchen, Skip was again tempted to talk about Harvey, this time to his father.

"Well, son," said the Reverend Clinton Ellis — he happened to be in the kitchen at the time, in the vicinity of the oven; he loved baked scallops the way Harvey's mother fixed them, and could never resist peeking in at them and sniffing their aroma — "how did it go today?"

26

"Fine, Dad. I made two dollars taking a couple of men out to the islands."

"To the islands? To look at Ben's cabin, you mean?"

"Well, yes, that was part of it."

Skip described the men and the trip.

"Well, well. I hope Ben gets a couple of weeks' rent out of them," said Mr. Ellis, who was truly a Christian man and always on the lookout for the welfare of his flock, both spiritual and physical. Old Ben Doane didn't make it to church very often — mostly for funerals — but he and the parson were good friends all the same. The first two big lobsters of the season were always dropped off at the parsonage.

Again, for a moment, it was on the tip of Skip's tongue to say something about Harvey. In a way his father deserved to know about it, since it was he who had talked Harvey out of trouble after the pieces-of-eight episode. Only his eloquence had succeeded in calming down old Ephraim Fairchild and coaxing him off the warpath. Otherwise, the banker would have hung Harvey's scalp on his belt for sure.

"Dad, that crazy Harvey —" Skip began, and then stopped.

"What about Harvey, son?"

"Oh . . . he's really a character, that's all," said Skip lamely. Once again he decided there was no use getting anybody else worried about his friend when maybe nothing would come of the whole business anyhow.

"Has he been up to something new?" asked Mr. Ellis, alarmed.

"No, not exactly. It's just that he sure is one of a kind. There's nobody else quite like him."

27

"I won't argue with you there," declared Mr. Ellis with feeling. "But basically he's a fine boy with a brilliant mind, and I'm sure he'll make his mark." The minister chuckled. "I just hope he won't make it on all the rest of us!"

The Sou'wester Inn was located on Front Street, the street nearest the harbor. A few doors up Front Street, across the way, a sign in front of a snug old cottage announced that Ben Doane had NATIVE LOBSTERS FOR SALE.

Harvey had just finished waxing the floor in the entry hall of the inn when he happened to look out the door in time to see a car pull up in front of Ben's cottage. As a matter of fact, he did not just happen to look out, he had been watching pretty carefully ever since he had seen Ben's old pick-up truck turn into the driveway.

Two other cars had already stopped, but they were people Harvey knew, local people who were probably stopping to buy lobsters. When the third car stopped, however, Harvey saw what he had been waiting for.

He watched with keen interest while the car's occupants approached the cottage. At that point his Aunt Sarah called him to supper, but she had to call him twice before he heard. When he did come to the table, out in the big kitchen where the family ate, he was thinking so hard that he blundered into a chair and barked his shin.

"Land sakes, Harvey, are you a million miles away again?" demanded his aunt. She sighed sharply. "I never saw such a boy in all my born days."

"Sorry, Aunt Sarah," said Harvey, chuckling apologetically

28

in spite of the pain that had him hopping around on one foot. Harvey never got mad about the whacks he sometimes gave himself on his head and shins and elbows when his mind was elsewhere and he was not watching where he was going. He seemed to regard it as the price he had to pay for the use of an unusually active brain.

"What's on your mind now?"

"Nothing special. Aunt Sarah, is it all right if I get together with Skip for a few minutes after we finish doing the dishes tonight?"

"I suppose so, if your uncle hasn't got something he wants done."

As soon as he could, after supper, Harvey telephoned Skip.

Skip frowned as he listened to Harvey. He was sorry to hear the strangers had turned up again, but his curiosity was aroused just as Harvey's was.

"They went to see Ben, huh?" said Skip. "All right, I'll come over as soon as I can, and we'll go tell Ben about our trip and see if they rented the cabin."

A few minutes later he walked down the hill to the Sou'-wester Inn. Harvey was waiting outside.

"Now remember, Harvey, don't you say anything funny about Doc and the professor."

"I'll let you do the talking, Skip."

Together they hurried across the street to Ben Doane's, and found him out in his back yard mending a lobster pot.

Ben Doane was over seventy years old, and a New Englander through and through. An ancestor of his had settled

29

in Goose Harbor more than two hundred years ago, and the Doanes were still there. People often wondered how Ben managed to stay so healthy and hardy and tend a string of lobster pots by himself every day of the season. "Well," someone had once figured it out, "one thing is sure, he doesn't wear himself out talking." Ben was a man of few words.

"Evening, Mr. Doane," said Skip and Harvey as they walked around into his back yard.

Ben looked up and nodded.

"Evening, boys."

"Good lobstering today?"

"Got a few."

"That's good. Mr. Doane, two men turned up today and hired me to take them out to the islands," began Skip.

"Did, eh?"

"Yep. Fat man named Dr. Dillingham, and another man named Professor Santos."

Ben grunted, and continued to work on the lobster pot. It was a cagelike box, made of wood laths, with a funnel-shaped net through which lobsters could crawl into the box to get at the bait inside.

"We put in at Doane Island and walked all over it, and they looked in the cabin windows to see what it was like," Skip went on. "Then we went on over to Tree House Island and went ashore there, too. They said they were ornithologists."

"Orney-whatsits?"

"They study birds."

Ben snorted, which was generally as near as he came to laughter.

"Eph Fairchild and his Birdbrains'll like that."

The boys laughed, and agreed.

"They're working for some scientific foundation," Skip added.

"That so?"

"Yep. Professor Santos is from some foreign university."

"Santiago," said Harvey. "Cuba."

"You think he's a Cuban, Harve?" asked Skip.

"Maybe. But he could be from some place else in Central America or South America."

31

"Well, anyway, we thought we ought to come and tell you about taking them out there," Skip told Ben. "They said they might be wanting to rent your cabin for a week or so."

"Did they, now?"

"Yep. So we were hoping they would."

"Well, that's mighty neighborly of you, boys." The old man nodded, and got up to go into his shed for a hammer. The boys tagged along behind, glancing at each other and wondering what to say next.

Harvey cleared his throat.

"I happened to be outside just before supper, and saw them stop here, so I suppose they found you all right."

"Yep," said Ben. "They found me."

He picked up the hammer and went outside again. The boys exchanged another frustrated glance. It didn't look as if Ben was going to have anything more to say on the subject.

Harvey could not quite restrain himself.

"Well, what happened, Mr. Doane? Did they . . ."

He stopped as the old man swung around and glowered at him. Harvey reddened, remembering that it was none of his business if Ben did not choose to talk about it further.

" 'Scuse me," he mumbled, and shot a flustered glance at his friend. "Well, I guess we'll be going along, huh, Skip?"

"Yes, g'night, Mr. Doane."

Ben grunted.

They had started to walk away when a loud snort stopped them in their tracks. They turned to find the old man's eyes twinkling with mischief.

"Hold on. Can't stand to see you suffer," he said. "They rented both islands from me, lock, stock 'n' barrel, for scientific purposes, starting tomorrow. What's more, paid me for a week in advance!"

3

ONCE BEN DOANE had had his fun with the boys, he told them the whole story. He said the two men planned to return the next afternoon and set themselves up out on Doane Island.

"How are they planning to get back and forth?" asked Skip.

"By boat," said Ben dryly.

Skip grinned. "Well, I didn't figure they'd swim — but *what* boat?"

"They're bringing one."

The boys were down on the beach the next afternoon watching Lee Rand put the final coat of anti-fouling paint on the upturned bottom of his twelve-footer when the men appeared. Rolling along behind their car was a boat trailer with an inboard motorboat on it.

Doc noticed the boys at once. He waved and smiled. Professor Santos nodded.

The professor backed the trailer expertly off the road onto the beach without getting the car wheels off into soft sand. The men climbed out and prepared to unhitch the trailer and roll it down to the water's edge.

34

"Come on, let's give 'em a hand," said Skip, and the boys ran up to help.

"Hello again, lads," said the smiling fat man. "Want to help us launch the *Leeway*? Isn't she a little beauty? Lent by a friend of the Foundation for the duration of our survey. Not bad, eh?"

"I'll say not," said Skip, running his hand over her short mahogany deck. "What kind of motor has she got?"

"I don't know, you'll have to tell me," said Doc, laughing. "You can look her over later on, if you'd like to. Got the hitch unhooked there, Professor? Good, let's roll her down."

Lee put down his brush and came over to join them as they walked the trailer down the beach. With the professor managing the winch, the rest of them guided the boat off the trailer onto the sand and then dragged her into the water. Professor Santos hopped aboard, started the motor, and ran the boat over alongside the float.

When the *Leeway* had been launched, Skip thought to introduce Lee Rand to Doc. He and Harvey had already told Lee the bare facts about the newcomers.

"An artist, eh?" said Doc, shaking hands. "I hope I'll have a chance to see some of your work while we're here, although on the salaries we poor research people are paid I can't promise I'll be able to buy any paintings. Well, now, I think we'll load up and take a run out to the island. We'll probably have to make three trips to get all our stuff out there. The car's piled high with it."

They all helped carry a wide assortment of suitcases, bundles, cases, equipment, and stores down to the boat.

35

"I'd sure like to know what's in this box," muttered Harvey, as he and Skip carried down a load.

"Don't be so nosy," growled Skip. Just to put Harvey in his place, he added, "It's full of pieces of eight, I'm sure."

"Not heavy enough," Harvey retorted cheerfully. He was a hard guy to down.

The boat was quickly loaded.

"Many hands make light work, as they say," remarked Doc. "It's mighty nice of you lads to give us a hand this way. I guess that's enough for now — remember, there's still me to go in the boat, and we don't want to sink. So we'll shove off, and be back shortly."

When the *Leeway* had moved out into the channel, with the professor at the wheel and Doc waving to them genially, the boys and Lee returned to his boat.

"Well, he's quite a character, isn't he?" said Lee.

"Sure is," said Harvey, staring after the *Leeway*. "What do you think of him, Lee?"

"Hard to say, offhand. That Professor Santos doesn't have much to say, does he?"

"I don't think he speaks much English," said Skip.

By the time Lee had finished painting his boat, the two men were back again. Doc called to the boys.

"Say, maybe you lads would like to make a couple of bucks taking a load out for us? That way we'd only have to make one more run."

"At your service, Doc," said Skip. He and Harvey began loading up the *Fifteen* under the fat man's direction.

"Go get rid of the car and trailer, Professor," said Doc,

when everything was out of the car and into the boats. "Mr. Doane's letting us park in his yard," he explained.

When the professor returned, the boys followed the *Leeway* out to the island. There they helped carry everything into the cabin.

"That's great, lads," said Doc. He handed Skip four dollar bills, two of which Skip immediately passed on to Harvey.

"No, it's your boat," protested Harvey.

"Never mind that. You did as much work as I did, so take it."

Doc turned to the professor. "Fair and square. I like that." He turned back to the boys jovially. "Well, many thanks, lads, I guess that does it."

As soon as they were on their way back to the harbor, Harvey turned eagerly to Skip. The large eyes behind his thick glasses were gleaming with excitement.

"Guess what I saw out there!"

"What?"

"Well, when I came up with one load of stuff, Doc told me to put it in the bedroom. So I walked on through to the bedroom, and when I went in the professor was just putting a gun away in a drawer."

"Now, wait a minute! That sounds just like something Harvey Harding would think up."

"No, I'm not kidding. He didn't think I saw him, and I pretended not to notice. He was mad, and said, 'In there! In there!' — pointing to the living room. Doc had told me to take my load to the bedroom. I guess the professor hadn't been expecting that."

"H'm. Well, so he was putting a gun away. Maybe they use it to kill birds with, when they need specimens."

"A revolver?"

Skip shrugged uneasily.

"Scientists collecting specimens of birds use small shells with a light charge," Harvey added.

"Well, maybe they feel they need a gun for protection, alone out there on the island."

"Now who's making up stuff?" scoffed Harvey. "Who's going to bother anybody around here? I don't think they have to worry much about pirates or holdup men out there."

"I'll admit, there hasn't been a stagecoach robbed out on Doane Island in years," said Skip, grinning. "Well, I don't know what the professor is doing with a revolver, but there's probably some good reason for it."

"Yes, and I wish I knew what it is," said Harvey.

As might be expected in a bird-loving community such as Goose Harbor, there was quite a stir over the arrival of the ornithologists. Every one of the town's eleven hundred inhabitants knew they had rented the islands for their research work before they had even returned with the *Leeway* and their supplies.

Since the Goose Harbor Bird Study Club's regular biweekly meeting happened to be scheduled for this very evening, it immediately occurred to several of the members that Dr. Dillingham and Professor Santos should be invited to attend and perhaps say a few words to the group.

Each of these several members telephoned the bank and told their idea to Ephraim Fairchild, who informed them that he had already thought of the same idea himself. He said he would see to it the two visitors were invited.

Happening to meet the minister on the street, Mr. Eph was reminded of a good way to reach the visitors.

"Clint, your boy has his new boat in the water now, hasn't he? I wonder if you'd ask him to run a message out to the gentlemen on Doane Island for the Bird Study Club?"

A couple of hours later Skip and Harvey were on their way to Doane Island with a letter addressed in old Mr. Fairchild's squiggly handwriting. Doc came smiling down to the wharf to meet them. His fat body was clothed in a loud shirt and khaki bermudas, and a pair of field glasses hung around his neck. Up at the cabin, Professor Santos appeared at the door and stood watching them. There was no welcoming look on his face.

"Well, lads, nice to see you again," said Doc. "In fact, I was just thinking about you. We've got a problem I'm sure you can help us with. Come ashore, and let's have a chat."

Skip glanced at Harvey, but he was already scrambling onto the wharf to make the *Fifteen* fast. Skip secured the stern line and followed him. Doc sat down on a plank that had been nailed to two piles to form a rough bench at the head of the wharf. He waved a hand about him and chuckled.

"Pull up a chair and sit down, lads," he said, and the boys sat down cross-legged on the wharf in front of him. "Now then. Here's our problem. For about a week we're going to want the birds on these islands to be disturbed as little as possible. Now, I judge from that tree house over on the small island that the local kids come out here to play sometimes?"

"That's right. Mostly on the small island, though. Oh, sometimes they fool around out here, too, but everybody knows Ben Doane, and nobody ever bothers anything. They leave the cabin alone, and all."

"I see. For one thing, it wouldn't be hard to find out which kids had been out here, I guess, eh? Well, that's fine. However, for just this week we would appreciate it if the birds could be absolutely undisturbed. Now, you're two of the older boys here in Goose Harbor, aren't you? I imagine the younger boys look up to you, don't they? I imagine that what you say goes, eh?"

"Well, yes, I suppose so," said Skip. It happened to be quite true, of course — being the best boat-handler, swimmer, and all-around athlete among Goose Harbor's kids, Skip was their unofficial leader.

"Well, then," Doc went on, "if you spread the word around that we would like everyone to stay clear of the islands for just a week or so, I imagine they'd go along, wouldn't they?"

"Yes, I guess they would. Matter of fact, there aren't many boats in the water yet anyway. The only kid I know of that's been out to Tree House Island so far is Gumbo Phillips — right, Harvey?"

"That's right, Skip."

"Gumbo?" Doc laughed at the nickname. The bright sunshine gleamed on his plump cheeks as he tipped his head back, and then his small eyes bored into Skip again. "And who is Gumbo Phillips?"

"Oh, he's a crazy little kid with a canoe. He's only twelve, but he paddles that thing everywhere — even out to the island, given a calm day."

"I see. Well, and do you think you could talk to Gumbo?"

"Sure. He'll cooperate."

"Good. Gumbo!" Doc laughed again, a rich, rumbling fat man's laugh. "And where did he get a nickname like that? A lover of chicken gumbo soup, I suppose?"

"No, actually he got it because he's always chewing bubble gum."

"Oh. I see. Well, if you'll take care of Gumbo and any other kids who might otherwise visit the islands, we'll very

41

much appreciate it. By the way — what brought *you* out here?"

Skip produced the letter.

"Mr. Fairchild asked us to bring you this."

"Mr. Fairchild?"

"Ephraim Fairchild. He's president of the bank."

"Oh, a banker, eh? Well, I don't think I owe him any money, so I'll open his letter," said Doc, chuckling. He read the letter and glanced around at the professor, who had been watching silently from the doorway the whole time. "Well, well! Gracious invitation to attend the local bird study club meeting this evening. I like that." He turned back to the boys. "Tell Mr. Fairchild we'll be delighted to attend, will you?"

Behind him, Professor Santos started forward frowning angrily. It was startling to have him move after standing quietly for so long.

"No, no!" he said. "No meeting!"

Doc glanced at him still smiling, but his eyes had gone very small.

"It starts at eight-thirty. We can be back by ten-thirty." His face was bland again as he turned to the boys. "We have to be up very early, of course, so the professor doesn't like to stay up late. But naturally we're glad to put ourselves out a little for a club that shares our serious interest in birds. Furthermore, they can probably help us, too. Does the club have many members?"

"Oh, yes."

"Would you say it was an influential club?"

Skip grinned. "Any club Eph Fairchild belongs to is influential, and besides him a lot of other important people belong."

"Splendid, splendid. Then no doubt they can help me get adult cooperation as far as the islands are concerned. I'll mention the matter at the meeting tonight." He rose to his feet. "Well, thanks for coming out, lads, and give Mr. Fairchild my message, will you?"

The boys untied the *Fifteen* and Skip backed her away from the wharf. Doc waved good-by, and then turned to speak to the professor. Although Skip could see only a corner of his round face, he got the impression that Doc was no longer smiling. And Professor Santos looked as though he were being told off properly.

"Looks as if Doc's explaining who's boss around there," remarked Harvey. "Say, that was interesting. Very interesting. I wonder what the professor's real reason is for not wanting to go to the meeting?"

Skip frowned at him.

"Harvey, you are the most suspicious guy I ever knew!"

"Well? Were you satisfied with Doc's explanation?"

"Well . . . it was logical enough . . ."

"Yes, but the way the professor acted . . . and Doc got hot under the collar for a minute there, too, which is strange. Why get sore about such a little thing, if that's all there is to it? And another thing — why don't they want anybody on the islands for a week?"

"Well, now, *that* part at least made sense."

"Maybe. But if one thing is fishy, another thing may be, too." Harvey was silent for a moment, thinking. He sat with

43

his hands on his knobby knees, staring back at the island as though trying to penetrate its secrets by the sheer force of intense concentration. Finally he spoke again. "Say, you know what? I'd like to go to the Birdbrains' meeting tonight and hear what Doc has to say. Think they'd let us come?"

"Why, sure. I don't know why not. They always say their meetings are open to the public."

"Well, just to make sure, why don't you ask Mr. Eph when we get to the bank? He can hardly refuse, for that matter, after we've done him and the club a favor."

"That's true. All right, I'll ask him," said Skip, and then frowned at his friend again and poked him in his thin ribs. "Doggonit, now you've got me curious, too!"

The old banker was surprised at their request, but not displeased. In fact, he looked as nearly pleased as he ever did about anything.

"Certainly you can come. We're anxious to have a good turnout for our visitors, so the more the merrier. Glad to see you boys taking an interest in something serious for a change," he declared, and looked over his glasses meaningfully at Harvey. "Specially you, young fellow!"

At the corner of Front Street and Sea Street stood Liberty Hall, the white frame building in which most public meetings in Goose Harbor were held. When Skip and Harvey entered the building shortly before 8:30, they found Dr. Dillingham and Professor Santos already there, standing in the midst of a group of club members at the front of the

44

room while Eph Fairchild introduced them around the circle. Doc was his usual beaming self as he shook hands, and even the professor seemed to be making some effort to look pleasant, though he said very little.

When Doc noticed that the boys had come in, he looked pleased and walked over to them.

"Well, well, my young friends! Lads, I take this as a real compliment," he declared, putting his small, neat hands on their shoulders. "And did you pass the word around to the other lads about the islands?"

"We've spoken to several kids already," nodded Skip.

"How about the lad with the canoe? Gumbo, wasn't that his name?"

"That's right. We weren't able to find him, but we left word for him."

"Good. You're a great help, and I appreciate it."

All of Goose Harbor's prominent bird watchers were on hand, plus a number of persons who did not usually take more than average interest in birds, but who were curious to see the visiting scientists. Even Lee Rand turned up, with a sketch pad under his arm, and took a seat in the back row with Skip and Harvey. A minute or two later Mary Fairchild arrived. She stood looking around as though there were almost no seats left, and then turned to Lee.

"Pardon me, is this seat taken?" she murmured, pointing to the one beside him.

"Well, I *was* saving it for your grandfather," murmured Lee, "but I don't think he's going to want it, so you may have it."

The boys snickered, and Mary frowned as she sat down beside them.

"That'll be enough out of you two," she declared sternly.

They grinned at her broadly, but her grandfather didn't. He glared as he saw that Mary was sitting with Lee, but Lee was busy drawing a funny sketch of the old man and didn't seem to notice, and Mary pretended she didn't notice either. Poor old Mr. Eph was dissatisfied with life, as usual, anyway. He peered irritably through a side window at the night sky.

"Dad-blame the luck!" he complained. "Attendance likely to be held down some by this threatening weather."

Lightning was flashing in the northwest, and an uneasy breeze was stirring the leaves of the trees.

"Yes, it looks as if we may get a squall later on," said Doc. "In fact, if you don't mind, I hope you'll let me say a few words early in the meeting so we can head back to the island. Much as I'd enjoy staying through all of your meeting, I wouldn't like to get caught in a storm."

"By all means," said Mr. Eph. "We'll get started right away."

He called the meeting to order, waited impatiently until a few late-comers had taken seats, and remarked that in spite of the threatening weather fifty-three persons were present.

"We'd probably have had a record turnout if the night had stayed nice," he concluded mournfully. "We'll dispense with the reading of the minutes until later, Miss Gurnet," he told the birdlike little old lady who had been the club's secretary for forty years. "We'll get right on to our visitors. Ladies and gentlemen, by now you all know who our distinguished visitors are — Dr. Dillingham and Professor Santos. They're here to carry on ornithological research on the islands for a scientific foundation, and I'm sure Dr. Dillingham will tell us more about that in the course of his talk. So without further ado I'll present Dr. Dillingham, who will speak to us on the topic, 'Bird Life on the Islands of the Atlantic Coast.' Dr. Dillingham."

Doc arose to warm applause, and began by intoducing his colleague.

"Professor Santos is from the University of Santiago in Cuba. Since he speaks very little English, he's going to let me do the talking tonight — I usually do most of the talking wherever I am, anyway," joked Doc, and winked as the audience laughed. "Now, to begin with, I'm sorry I can't give you a detailed account of the research work we're involved in at the moment, but the entire project is being done very quietly, for fear that curiosity will draw people to some of the islands involved and disturb bird life there. In that connection, I'd like to enlist the help of this club in keeping everyone off the islands during the next week or so. I hardly need explain the importance of this to a group such as yours. We have already been promised the help of my young friends, Skip Ellis and Harvey Harding, in keeping the youngsters off the islands, so perhaps you folks can take care of the grownups."

It flustered Skip a trifle to have everybody glance around at him when Doc mentioned them, but Harvey scarcely seemed to notice. He was concentrating on Doc's every word and movement.

Mr. Eph rose to respond to Doc's appeal. With his words

47

backed by an approving murmur from the audience, and his fierce old eyes flashing a general warning in all directions, he assured Doc they would see to it in the name of science that nobody did any trespassing on the islands.

"Thank you. That's good news to us, you may be sure," Doc declared. "You'd be surprised how hard it is to get co-operation sometimes in less enlightened communities that don't have strong, scientific-minded groups such as your club to help out. Knowing how serious and dedicated you are, I wish I could take you a little more on the inside of our project and tell you about the Foundation — and personally I can't see what harm it would do. However, I don't set the Foundation's policies, and for the present the policy is that it's to remain anonymous. Well, you can't argue with a family that gives millions for scientific research if that's the way they want it, so . . ." Doc shrugged, and his audience murmured and nodded understandingly. "However, I can assure you that when our whole story can be told, I will see to it that your club is included among the scientific societies to be notified in advance of the general public," he added, causing even Mr. Eph to look enormously proud.

Next Dr. Dillingham launched into his talk, and gave a very interesting account of several islands and of the birds to be found on them. Lee drew a number of sketches of Doc while he talked. When Doc had finished, and had been suitably thanked by Mr. Eph on behalf of the entire gathering, he and Professor Santos excused themselves and left.

"Shall we stay for the rest of the meeting?" Harvey whispered to Skip as the group settled down to hear Miss

48

Gurnet's customary reading of the minutes of the last meeting.

"Gee, I don't know. Do you think we can sneak out?"

"Well," whispered Harvey, "we can try."

"Maybe we ought to stay a while and build up your credit with Mr. Eph."

Harvey shrugged. "Well, all right, if you don't mind. We're here, I suppose we may as well stay."

They sat back in their seats and waited for Miss Gurnet to finish her minutes. Next came the treasurer's report from Mr. Filkins and the news that the present balance in the club's treasury was three hundred and sixty-eight dollars and forty-two cents. This was followed by a report from the Shore Birds Protection Committee, which was given by Ralph Lynch, the hardware man. Skip covered a yawn and glanced at Harvey.

"Maybe Mr. Eph won't notice if we're quiet enough," he whispered. He leaned forward and whispered to Mary. "Think it would be all right if we left now?"

Mary grinned. "I think you're crazy if you don't!" she whispered.

Before they could act on her advice, however, an outside influence took care of matters.

"Psst!"

The sound came from the window beside them. They glanced out to see Gumbo Phillips craning his neck to look in at them. He beckoned urgently.

"Skip! C'mere!" he hissed in a loud whisper that caused heads to turn all over the room, including Mr. Eph's. He

49

cleared his throat in an annoyed way as the boys, after signaling to Gumbo to be quiet, rose and tiptoed out.

"What's the matter with you, anyway?" Skip demanded of Gumbo as they came outside. Gumbo was fidgety with excitement, and looked worried. He was so small he made even Harvey seem large, but he made up for his small size by having enormous energy.

Right now, however, he was so concerned with whatever was on his mind that he wasn't even chewing his usual bubble gum.

"Hey, I just heard about how we're not supposed to go out to the islands any more," he said, "and that reminded me!"

"Reminded you of what?"

"Harvey's telescope."

"What about my telescope?"

"Well, when you lent it to me the other day to study stars with, I took it out to Tree House Island that night."

"Oh. Well, that doesn't matter. It's from now on that counts, just this week."

"I know, but I forgot and left your telescope up in the tree house!"

"What!"

"Gee, I'm sorry, Harv. I only just remembered now. And we got to get it, because it's going to rain, and rain won't do your 'scope any good."

"It sure won't," agreed Harvey. It was one he had built himself, and the tubes were made of cardboard which he had painted black. As a telescope it worked very well, but it was certainly not waterproof. "Well, Skip? What'll we do?"

"Maybe Doc hasn't shoved off yet. Let's see if we can catch them!"

4

By the time they reached the town wharf, however, the *Leeway* was already out near the harbor entrance. As scudding clouds raced past a full moon and left it in the open for a moment, they could see a black dot and her white wake on the water out off the Point.

"Well, I guess we'd better let my 'scope go and take a chance on the weather," said Harvey as they stood in a line on the beach.

Skip knew he was saying it because he didn't have a boat of his own and didn't want to risk getting Skip and the *Fifteen* into trouble.

"The heck with that. Listen, we're not going to hurt anything," he said. He began to take off his shoes and socks and roll up his pants. "We can run out there and pick up your telescope and tell them about it tomorrow. Doc'll understand. Come on!"

Gumbo was all set to go along, but Skip shooed him off.

"Out!" he said, thumbing him out of the *Fifteen*. "If there's any trouble over this, there's no use in your being in it, too."

Gumbo was outraged.

"What do you mean? It's my fault you have to go out there at all, so I got more right to get in trouble than anybody!"

"Out!" repeated Skip, jerking his thumb again.

"What a dirty trick," grumbled Gumbo, as he went reluctantly over the side and waded back onto the beach. Skip started the motor, and they left him standing forlornly at the water's edge.

In the moonlight they could still see the *Leeway*'s wake far ahead of them as they cruised out of the harbor. As soon as they cleared the entrance Skip increased speed and set a course straight for Tree House Island.

"I hope none of the Birdbrains leave the meeting early and see a boat out here heading for the island," said Harvey. "I wish that darn moon weren't so bright."

"Don't worry. We'll explain all about it tomorrow, if we have to."

In the northwest, thunder continued to mutter distantly, and they could see lightning flashes low on the horizon, but the storm did not seem to be moving any closer.

"What did you think of Doc's talk?" asked Skip. "You'll have to admit, he knows his birds."

"Yes, he sure seems to. It was a good talk."

"Are you convinced he's on the level, then?"

"No."

"Well, for Pete's sake, why not?"

"He just doesn't ring true to me. I'd like to know more about this foundation he's working for."

"Well, I don't see anything so unusual about that — his

53

not being able to tell us all about it, I mean. Lots of scientific outfits try to duck publicity while they're working on a project. And anyway, if even a shrewd old geezer like Mr. Eph is willing to accept Doc and the professor, why shouldn't you?"

"Listen, Mr. Eph and all the other Birdbrains are delighted to have a couple of scientists turn up. They *want* to believe in Doc and the professor. I'll admit that when you're suspicious to begin with, everything that happens makes you more suspicious, but I still wonder about those two. Maybe I'm all wet. I even hope I am. However, we'll see."

The tiny strip of beach that was sandwiched between the rocks on the shoreward side of Tree House Island gleamed brightly in the moonlight every time the string of ragged clouds thinned enough to let the moon show its round face. The solitary big tree and the tree house stood out blackly. Dark leaves tossed restlessly about the weathered boards. Even some of the upper cross-sticks that were nailed to the tree trunk to form the ladder showed up dimly.

Skip slowed the *Fifteen*. Harvey crouched in the bow ready to leap ashore the instant she touched the sand.

"Make it snappy, now, Harv."

"I will."

The keel grated softly. Harvey swung over the side, tugged the bow in to hold the boat ashore, and ran quickly up toward the tall tree standing on the high ground in the center of the little island. Skip could see him dimly, following the path through the low underbrush that led up to the tree house.

54

He watched expectantly for the sight of Harvey silhouetted against the sky as he climbed the tree, but Harvey did not appear. Skip waited with growing impatience, anxious to make their trespassing on the island as brief as possible.

"What's keeping that guy, anyway?" he growled to himself. Finally he went over the side to go check on his unpredictable friend.

As he stepped out, a gash in the sand at the water's edge nearby caught his eye. He stopped to study it, then walked thoughtfully up the beach and set the anchor in the sand. He trotted along the path to the tree house, and found Harvey down on his knees, examining the ground.

"Hey, what are you doing?"

"Something funny here, Skip. I never heard of digging for birds."

"What do you mean?"

"They've been probing the ground all around here with a rod of some kind, and they've dug several holes and filled them up again."

Skip crouched beside Harvey for a look.

"Well, I'll be darned. What do you suppose they could be digging for?"

"That's what I'd like to know." Harvey's big black-rimmed glasses flashed in the moonlight, almost as though his eyes had lighted up, and Skip knew the wheels were turning briskly in his active mind.

"By the way, Harv, I just noticed a keel mark in the sand."

"I saw it," nodded Harvey.

"Might know you wouldn't miss anything!"

56

"I was going to point it out to you when I got back. I meant to hurry as fast as I could, until these diggings pulled me up short. What do you think about that mark?"

"Well, it's not our keel mark from the other day, because we brought them out here at dead low tide."

"That's right. And you notice it's almost even with where we hit the beach just now."

"Yeah. Which means they were here just about as much ahead of low tide this afternoon as we're here after it. Low tide was at seven-thirty tonight, and it's now nine-thirty. So they were here around five o'clock."

"Right. Now the question is, what were they doing here this afternoon, probing and digging? What were they looking for? Is there a new species of underground birds we don't know about?"

Skip grinned. "Well, I don't know, but let's not get carried away. There may be some good scientific reason for this digging they're doing."

"Maybe so — but as long as we're here, and as long as we've got this nice bright moonlight to work by, I want to look all around."

"Well, okay, but let's not be too long about it, Harv. With this strong offshore wind they may have heard us coming out."

They tramped all over the island, but only near the center did they find any signs of digging. All around them the underbrush sighed and rustled as the wind picked up in ever stronger gusts. A jagged flash of lightning split the sky nearby, and thunder rolled its tardy warning across the waters.

57

"Hey, that's too close for comfort. We'd better hurry, Harv. Storm's really moving this way now."

"Okay, let's go get my telescope and run for it."

They had returned to the foot of the big tree again when Skip seized Harvey's arm.

"Hey! Listen!"

They froze. Distinctly they could hear the sound of a motor.

"Quick! Hop up and get that 'scope."

As thin and bony and loose-limbed as he was, Harvey sometimes gave the impression of being temporarily wired together, but he was surprisingly quick of movement when he had to be. He scampered up to the tree house in a flash.

He grabbed the telescope and started down. One instant there was only moonlight. The next instant Harvey was blinking like an owl in the circle of a bright hard beam. A powerful searchlight had stabbed through the night air and impaled him against the tree house. He hung there, blinking, with the telescope in his hand.

For a moment the beam stayed on him, as relentlessly as a stream of bullets. Then it winked off. The spell broken, Harvey dropped quickly down the ladder and exchanged a wild-eyed look with Skip.

"Gosh, where did they come from?" asked Skip.

"I don't know. All at once, there they were, in the *Leeway*, just coming around the lee of the island."

"What'll we say?"

"Just tell them the truth, that's all."

They walked down the path to the tiny beach. The *Leeway* rounded into the miniature cove. Again the powerful searchlight bit through the darkness, full into their eyes, half blinding them as they stumbled down the path. The boat's prow sliced into the sand as it coasted in, and they could see the vast bulk of the fat man rise up. Behind him lightning flashed in a huge, evil fork, illuminating the bloated figure for an instant and giving it a strangely sinister look. Thunder rolled toward them and the wind shrieked at it.

Doc stepped into the water and stood beside the searchlight mounted on the coaming of the boat.

"Well, well, well!" His voice was tight with controlled fury. "And what have we here?"

"I'm sorry, Doc," said Skip, "we —"

"Hardly an hour after you sat listening to me ask for cooperation. And after I asked you personally to help us out."

Professor Santos appeared on the other side of the boat and kept coming, up onto the beach, walking toward them. His dark face was hardly visible, but there was a menace in the small man's panther-like stride that sent a sudden chill down Skip's spine. It was as though he faced a cage door that had suddenly opened, setting loose something savage and violent.

But Doc's hand went out.

"Santos," he said sharply. The professor's long jaw set, and his eyes glittered dangerously, but he stopped.

Doc strolled toward them, and by the time he reached the boys he had his fury under control. He was even smiling his usual smile.

"Well, I suppose boys will be boys, but still I don't think you can blame us for being a trifle sore. I never expected to

59

find you up there at night with a glass, trying to spy on us."

"I wasn't trying to spy on you, Dr. Dillingham," said Harvey, and went on to explain about Gumbo and the telescope.

By the time he was through, Doc was managing to be almost affable.

"Gumbo again, eh? Well, all right. But I hope you two didn't tramp around here too much," he added, and his small eyes, narrowed to slits in the wind, studied Harvey with hard intensity as he spoke. "We're making some sample diggings in our study of the food supply here — worms and insects, that is — and that's one reason we want as little disturbance as possible."

Under Doc's close scrutiny, Harvey's expression betrayed enough embarrassment to make him suspect the truth. He chuckled in his rich, throaty way.

"So! You had a look around, eh? Well, curiosity can be a good thing, you know, but so can minding your own business. I hope you'll remember that. We won't say anything more about your trespassing this time, lads — but I do hope you'll be smart and not let it happen again. For one thing, Professor Santos here has the sort of excitable Latin temperament that's sometimes hard to restrain. He might make himself very unpleasant next time. So give us your cooperation from here on in, eh, lads?"

"Yes, sir," said Skip, with a glance at Harvey.

"We will, sir," said Harvey.

Doc turned to the professor, who was still staring at them with merciless eyes. "You see, Professor? They're really sorry. I like that." He glanced out at the water, which was kicking up under the gusts of wind. "You're going to have a wet trip in, lads. Think you can make it all right?"

"Oh, sure."

"Then get going."

Skip pulled the *Fifteen*'s anchor out of the sand and hurried down the beach, coiling the line as he went. When line and anchor were stowed away he swung aboard. Harvey shoved the boat free and hopped in over the bow as the *Fifteen* slid backwards away from the beach. Skip started the motor and headed her around.

Still standing in the beam of the searchlight, Doc waved a genial farewell and walked down to the *Leeway*. The professor stood by as impassively as an Indian, watching them unblinkingly. The boys waved, and Skip set a course for the harbor, giving the outboard all the speed he could in the rough sea that was rapidly making up. Behind them, the searchlight winked out.

Skip blew out a long breath, and for a moment the boys eyed each other silently.

"Well, chum, we really walked into it that time," said Skip finally.

"I wish they didn't have such a quiet boat. They were right on top of us before I heard a sound."

"Listen, with this offshore wind and the way the sea was making up, we wouldn't have heard the *Queen Mary*. Well, I just hope Doc doesn't say anything about this to Mr. Eph."

"I hope not, too."

They glanced back instinctively toward the island. A great fiery bolt of lightning ran from sky to sea like a giant white-hot wire, illuminating the water for an instant, and showing them the *Leeway* just moving away from the beach.

"There they go."

"Yep . . . listen, Harv, are you satisfied now that they're on the level?"

"Are you, Skip?"

"Well . . . no."

"Okay."

"I wouldn't blame them for being mad, but they were more than mad. For a minute there, I thought Professor Santos was really going to make trouble."

"So did I. And did you notice what Doc said when he stopped him? He didn't call him Professor. He just said 'Santos.' "

"Say, that's right. Of course, he did have a reasonable explanation for the digging."

"I figured he would have. That Doc is nobody's fool. You're not going to catch him off base easily. He'll have a reason ready for everything."

Skip dug a folded sheet of waterproof plastic out of the toolbox. "Here, wrap your 'scope in this. We might as well try to keep it dry, long's we've gone to all this trouble."

Another bolt of lightning hit the water, this time uncomfortably nearer. The *Fifteen* labored through heavy chops that were beginning to spin white spray from their crests and break over the bow of the boat to soak the boys.

"'Tain't a fit night for man nor beast out here — and us with good clothes on, too," remarked Harvey sadly, for both boys had dressed up to attend the meeting.

"It's getting sloppy, all right," agreed Skip, mopping his face with his sleeve. "I don't know but what I'll be glad when we're inside the harbor."

"I can think of worse places to be — including this," agreed Harvey. "Hand me the bailing can, Skip. I might as well get busy."

The howling wind slammed into the *Fifteen*, helping the sea to make her fight for every inch she made. The sky was black now, with only the lightning flashes to give them an occasional brilliant glimpse of the shoreline. Besides making headway, it was important to claw off the Point, where there were a number of big rocks that could make quick work of the *Fifteen*. Worse yet, the smell of rain was in the air now. Before long they would have that added hazard to contend with.

"In a minute visibility is going to be zero," predicted Skip.

"And relative humidity two hundred per cent," added Harv cheerfully, wiping off his glasses in a futile attempt to keep them clear.

"What are you doing that for?" snorted Skip.

"Want 'em to be nice and clean for the rain."

A lightning flash showed them a line of pockmarks moving swiftly toward them over the water, and then blackness and rain descended on them together. Rain fell in sheets and by the bucket. Working blindly, Harv bailed fast and furiously,

63

while Skip peered into the gray sheet of rain and used every scrap of his knowledge of sea and shoreline to calculate their position and judge how directly he dared to reach for the harbor mouth.

"Look!" shouted Harv, pointing as lightning flashed. Not more than a hundred yards abeam, the lethal mass that was Five Fathom Rock thrust its granite head above the white-caps that seethed about it.

"I see it," Skip replied. "It's too close for comfort, but so are some of these lightning bolts. I'm going to cut things a little fine and get inside as soon as I can."

In the tossing, churning sea and the buffeting wind it was next to impossible to hold the *Fifteen* on any course. Skip steered by instinct, meeting each wave and gust as a separate problem. Slowly the boat inched forward, while the pounding and grinding of surf hitting the Point sent chills down their backs.

Another flash showed Clam Rock fifty yards off their port bow.

"Almost there!" shouted Harv, who had looked over the top of his glasses in time to get a blurred vision of the rock.

The tip of the Point reached out for them greedily, and then they were around it and into the entrance. Even the harbor was choppy, but a millpond compared to what they had come through. They plodded up the harbor to the *Fifteen*'s mooring, bailed the boat as nearly dry as possible, and then came ashore in the old pram.

"How's the 'scope?" asked Skip. Wrapped tightly in the plastic sheet, it had made the trip far up in the bow, under

64

the forward thwart. Harvey carried it clutched against his chest now as Skip rowed in.

"All right, I hope. I'll see when we get in."

They carried the pram up the beach and tied her to a mooring-post. As they finished and turned to leave, a flashlight beam hit their eyes from the wharf.

"For Pete's sake!" muttered Skip. "Again?"

"Who's there?" called Harv.

Up on the wharf they could see the vague outlines of a jeep. A lean figure clad in oilskins and a sou'wester climbed out of it, flashlight in hand.

"Harvey Harding! Skip Ellis!" a stern old voice roared in indignant tones. "I want to see you two in the morning. Be at my office, eight-thirty sharp!" ordered Ephraim Fairchild, and climbed back in out of the wet.

Chilled and tired, wet as drowned rats, and every bit as miserable, Skip and Harvey stood watching the jeep back off the wharf, and then stared at each other.

"Well, boy, this is really our night," declared Skip at last.

"It sure is. And personally, I could have done without it," said Harvey — for his future looked blackest of all.

5

"But, Dad," said Skip, "don't you see? When we left the meeting we ran down to the beach and tried to catch them, but they had already left. There wasn't any point in running back to the hall to ask Mr. Eph for permission to go out there — he'd only have said he didn't have the right to give us permission, anyway. Besides, it didn't look as if there was time to go back, if we were going to beat the rain. So I figured the best thing to do was to get going and explain later."

The family conference was being held in his father's study. Out of his wet clothes now, wearing pajamas and robe, Skip sat on the edge of a chair sipping a mug of hot cocoa and watching his father pace up and down. Skip was not particularly fond of cocoa, but his mother put great faith in it as a safeguard after wettings, so he sometimes drank it rather than argue. His mother watched him silently. Curled up in the window seat, her arms folded, she looked on with a grave expression.

"Don't you see, Dad?" Skip repeated.

Mr. Ellis stopped, gazed down at his son, and sighed.

"Yes, I see. But I don't see why you couldn't have fetched

67

the telescope down from the tree house and been gone again in about two minutes, instead of taking so long that Dr. Dillingham came over to see who the trespassers were."

"I know. We meant to be quick about it, but then Harv noticed this digging they'd been doing, and we couldn't help being curious."

Mr. Ellis shook his head sadly.

"Oh, if only we could all learn to mind our own business in this world!"

"Still, it would have been hard not to be curious, dear," murmured Skip's mother.

"Spoken like a woman!" retorted her husband. "You put me in mind of a certain ancestor of yours named Eve who became so all-fired curious about an apple tree. The fact remains that Skip and Harvey knew they were on forbidden ground to begin with, so they should have restrained their curiosity."

Skip bit his lip and remained silent. Once again he was tempted to tell his father the whole story, and once again he resisted the temptation. What did the whole story add up to, when you came right down to it? A series of impressions, with not one shred of evidence for their suspicions that couldn't be explained away . . . Professor Santos had a gun. The two men had seemed angrier than necessary when they caught them trespassing. Professor Santos had looked ready to commit mayhem, but Doc had stopped him. All of which sounded exactly like the sort of thing people expected to hear from Harvey Harding. No, the worst thing they could do at this point would be to mention anything like that to anybody.

"Well, I don't know what Eph Fairchild will have to say to you two in the morning, but one thing is certain — he's going to be hopping mad," said Mr. Ellis. "I hope I won't have to try to talk Harvey out of trouble again. There's a limit to how many times I can turn the trick, you know."

Skip's father was a gentle man, but in no way a weak one. He could be a stern disciplinarian when he had to be. Skip knew he meant business when he put his hands behind his back, drew his brows together, and added, "And I don't want any more of this sort of thing, or I'll be forced to put severe restrictions on both you and your boat. Do you understand?"

By eight o'clock next morning Skip was on his way down the hill to the Sou'wester Inn. Harvey's Uncle Nate had already left on an errand, but his Aunt Sarah was on hand in the kitchen, washing the breakfast dishes while Harvey dried them.

Needless to say, she was doing a lot of worrying. Aunt Sarah was a worrier by nature. Although she seldom actually wrung her hands, she constantly looked as though she were about to do so. When everything was fine and dandy, she worried about the fact that things were going too well and something "turrible" was bound to happen. When trouble came, it only confirmed her gloomy expectations.

When Skip walked in, she gave him a mournful, how-could-you look.

"Skip Ellis, can't you two young'uns stay out of trouble for at least a week at a time, or are you going to keep me wor-

69

ried sick all summer?" she asked. "I swear, Harvey's uncle is just about ready to send him to Boston."

The subdued expression on Harvey's face showed that this was no idle threat. He dried a handful of silverware with elaborate care and made a great show of separating it with scrupulous accuracy as he put it in the silverware box. Usually, when the Brain was thinking while he worked, the knives were likely to end up in the spoons' section and the spoons among the forks.

"Well, we sure didn't mean any harm, Mrs. Harding," Skip assured Aunt Sarah, taking a dishtowel from the rack.

"I hope you can make Eph Fairchild believe that. But I swear, I'm half ready to agree with Harvey's uncle. He says, much as we can use Harvey's help around here, maybe the only way to keep him from getting into more trouble is to send him to stay with his Uncle Gilbert and Aunt Dorothy in Boston for a spell."

After a few more minutes of this melancholy talk, during which both Harvey and Skip dried dishes as fast as they could, the boys were able to slip away into the back yard for a conference before heading for the bank.

"You didn't say anything to them about your suspicions, did you?"

"Of course not." Harvey prowled back and forth, cracking his knuckles and staring into space with a deep frown. In his tee shirt and old white duck pants he looked like a scholarly sailor. His eyes had a faraway expression that made Skip check instinctively to see if there was anything in his friend's path he was likely to fall over or bark his shins on, since

70

Harvey himself would certainly never notice any obstacle at a time like this.

"What do my suspicions amount to so far, anyway? I don't even know what I'm suspicious *of* yet," Harvey went on. "So I had to sit and take my bawling out and say nothing, except to tell them the bare facts."

"Same here."

"Was your father mad, Skip?"

"Well, you know how he gets. Mad isn't exactly the description for it. I can tell you one thing, though — he promised me plenty of trouble if we get into any more messes."

"I'll bet. I expect he was pretty sore at me, too, after saving my neck last time."

"Well, he did say he didn't know how many more times he could turn the trick."

Harvey's thin face flushed.

"I'm sorry to have to worry him about this, Skip. I guess I should have thought about him before I went snooping around the island last night."

"Forget it. I went snooping, too." Skip glanced at the church clock, high on the hill but barely visible from the inn's back yard now that the trees had put out their leaves. "Well, guess we'd better get going."

"Okay, Skip. But how are we going to act?"

"Well, let's talk as little as possible, because anything we say will set Mr. Eph off just that much more."

"I expect you're right. So we'll just sit and take it again, I guess?"

"Yep."

Slowly, reluctantly, they left the safe harbor that was the inn's back yard and walked down the street toward the bank.

"Worse than going to the dentist, isn't it?"

"I hate to think what the old fire-eater's going to say."

The bank was not officially open for the day, so they had to knock on the glass doors that barred the public until 9 A.M. sharp. Their knock attracted the attention of the senior teller, Mr. Wixon, who was fussing around busily behind his window.

Mr. Wixon was a man who had a horror of making mistakes of any kind, large or small. On the rare occasions when his accounts were out by so much as a penny at the end of the banking day, he was a nervous wreck until he found the error. Naturally, then, he had long ago marked down Harvey Harding as one who would come to a bad end despite all his brains. In fact, if you had asked Mr. Wixon he would probably have given as his opinion that too many brains were a bad thing, just like too much of anything else.

He walked officiously to the door to let them in, and looked at them as though it were for the last time. Daniel probably received much the same sort of look from an attendant just before he stepped into the lions' den.

"He's in his office," said Mr. Wixon, and motioned them on.

Mr. Eph's private office was in a far corner of the bank, behind the tellers' cages and the two vice-presidents' desks. It was often referred to as the gloomiest room in Goose Harbor, especially by those who had ever gone there to ask for an extension on a loan. Its principal decoration was a

72

large portrait of the only native son who had ever looked grimmer than Mr. Eph — his great-grandfather, Obadiah Fairchild, the founder of the bank. The furnishings consisted of a ponderous desk and chairs of dark carved oak, and a thick red carpet. By comparison, the parlor of the Thacher Funeral Home down the street was a gay and giddy place.

The boys found Mr. Eph seated behind his desk waiting for them. The family resemblance between him and Great-grandfather Obadiah had never been stronger. When they entered he pulled out his old-fashioned hunting-case gold watch, snapped the case open, and gave it a sharp glance to make sure the boys were punctual.

"Good morning, Mr. Eph," they quavered. He snapped the watch shut and glared at them.

"Sit down," he said, indicating with a glance over the top of his glasses the two armchairs that stood stiffly at attention in front of his desk. The boys perched on the front edges of the chairs. Mr. Eph scratched away at some papers for a long moment, giving his visitors a chance to get thoroughly uncomfortable. Then he put his pen back in its holder, sat forward, and thrust his square old jaw at them.

"Now then. Just what were you two doing out on that island where you didn't have any business being?"

Before either boy could say anything, the old banker launched into a tirade.

"I was never so shocked in my life as I was when I realized it must be you two who were out there! There I was, driving home up the hill after the meeting, when all at once I saw a light on the water out by Near Island," declared Mr. Eph, using the old name, although most of Goose Harbor's adult population had taken to calling it Tree House Island along with the kids. "I went on home to get my oilskins and sou'wester and switch to my jeep. I got out my spyglass, and just before the weather closed in I caught a glimpse of a boat leaving the island. I drove down to the wharf to see who was coming in. When I checked moorings I saw your boat wasn't there. I could hardly believe my eyes. Not a quarter of an hour after Dr. Dillingham had finished asking for co-operation you two must have been on your way out to the island!"

He sat back with the air of a judge ready to pass sentence, but forcing himself to be scrupulous about the formalities first.

"Just what have you got to say for yourselves?"

Skip had agreed to do the talking. For one thing, the boys figured that Mr. Eph might listen to him a trifle less irritably than he would to Harvey.

"Well, to begin with, we heard this *pssst!* outside the window," he declared, and went on to tell Mr. Eph all about Gumbo and the telescope.

"It was my decision to go out there," he added. "I couldn't see what harm we could do just going ashore long enough to grab the telescope —"

"That's the way most folks get into messes!" snapped Mr. Eph. "They can't see any harm in doing things they shouldn't."

"Yes, sir. Well, anyway, we planned to tell Dr. Dillingham about it today."

Next came the hard part. Skip glanced at Harvey, gulped, and went on.

"But before we left the island, Dr. Dillingham and Professor Santos showed up. That was the light you saw — the searchlight on their boat."

"So! Caught you at it, did they?"

Up to this point Harvey had sat by, trying to seem as quiet and inoffensive as possible. Now, however, he surprised Skip by taking up the conversation.

"We stayed longer than we should have, Mr. Eph," he explained. "That was because I happened to notice some diggings that were none of our business."

"Diggings? What diggings?"

"Just some fresh diggings, sir, that were no concern of ours," said Harvey, dropping his eyes and looking very remorseful. "We had no right investigating them at all. We're very sorry."

"What are you talking about, boy?" demanded Mr. Eph, his large ears all but flapping with eagerness. "What kind of fresh diggings?"

Harvey suddenly looked up at him coolly.

"There! You see, Mr. Eph? You've got to admit, if you'd been out there and seen marks of digging all around the big tree, you'd have been curious, too! You couldn't help it — and neither could we!"

For a moment Mr. Eph could only sputter while his face went rooster-red. He rose with his eyes flashing, thrust his thumbs into the black suspenders under his seersucker jacket, and sat down again with a thump.

No matter what else anybody might say about the old banker, nobody could say he was not a fair man. After he had got through clearing his throat fiercely and considering Harvey's remarks from all sides, he accepted the truth of them.

"Very well!" he snapped finally. "Very well, let's say that these marks you saw would indeed provoke curiosity. You stopped and looked them over, did you?"

"Yes, sir," said Harvey, very meek again. "I'm ashamed to say we let our curiosity run away with us. We looked all over the island to see if they'd done any digging anywhere else."

"And had they?"

"No, sir."

"H'm. Digging." The old gentleman's lanky fingers drummed on his desk. "Why would they be digging? . . . Well, I'm sure there's some scientific reason behind it."

"Yes, sir. Dr. Dillingham explained about it. He said they were checking the food supply on the island — worms and insects, that is."

"Oh, yes. That makes sense." Mr. Eph sat back in his chair, obviously well satisfied with the explanation, and then looked at them severely again. "Another thing. I was about to go call out the Coast Guard to pick you up when you finally rounded the Point. I hope you won't be such dumb fools as to get caught out in weather like that again very soon."

"We hope not, too, Mr. Eph," agreed Skip.

An old wall clock ticked loudly while the old gentleman sat looking from one boy to the other. Then he leaned forward and shook a long forefinger at Harvey several times

76

while his throat rumbled ominously, clearing the way for a few final words of warning.

"Now then, Harvey Harding, this'll be about enough. You'd better not let that curiosity of yours make any more trouble for our visitors, because if you do you know what will be the consequences. I never thought I'd be giving you one more

chance after last night, but I'm going to. But this is your last one. Watch your step."

His eyebrows snarled together over the fierce eyes as he served this final notice on Harvey. Then he sat back.

"All right, that'll be all."

"Yes, sir," said the boys, and needed no second invitation

to depart. Skip moved quickly, but even so Harvey almost trod on his heels leaving the office and the bank.

When they were outside and safely out of sight and earshot of anybody in the bank, Skip allowed himself the pleasure of a whoop as he slapped Harvey on the back.

"Hey, Genius, that was great! I was ready to bust from trying not to laugh when you started working on Mr. Eph's curiosity!"

Harv grinned modestly. "Well, it suddenly occurred to me that maybe our best chance of getting off the hook was to make him see he'd have been just as curious as we were, if he'd been in our shoes."

"And it worked."

Harvey put one hand on his chest, flung the other out in a sweeping gesture, and quoted a line from his play *The Duke in the Dungeon*, which had been a great and gory success two summers before. "Ah, to smell the sweet air of freedom once again!" he cried.

"You said it, Duke," agreed Skip.

"Well, so much for that," said Harvey, and began to whistle in a low, thoughtful way.

"Yep, so much for that. You're in the clear with Mr. Eph, and from now on let's keep it that way."

"Yes, sure," muttered Harv absently.

"No more funny business."

Harvey did not reply.

"No more taking chances."

Again, no reply. Skip glanced at his friend, and saw that Harvey's mind was far, far away.

"Hey, are you listening to me?"

"What did you say?"

"Never mind. What are you cooking up now?"

"I'm thinking about what our next step should be."

"Our what? Hey now, listen —"

The faraway look left Harvey's eyes. They became sharp and clear as he stopped and turned to Skip.

"Yes, sir, I don't think there's any question about it. Our next step is to establish a watch on the Point, with my telescope, and watch Tree House Island day and night!"

6

"HARV, YOU'RE KIDDING!"

"No, I mean it."

"But you heard what Mr. Eph said."

"Yes, I heard."

"Then don't start playing with fire again!"

Harvey's big eyes searched Skip's face for a moment. He asked an abrupt question.

"Would you be willing just to walk away now and forget about Doc and the professor?"

Skip frowned. "Well, I won't say I'd forget about them, but —"

"You'd still be wondering about them, wouldn't you?"

"Well, yes. But look at it this way, Harv. Even if there is something fishy about them, what on earth could they be up to out on Tree House Island that could be so bad? Maybe whatever they're doing is harmless."

"Maybe. But they just don't look like harmless men to me. I haven't any idea yet as to what they might be up to, but I'll be uneasy until I know."

80

They started walking again, hands in their pockets, thoughtful scowls on their faces. When they reached Town Wharf Street they turned with one accord toward the water.

"Let's go out on the wharf," said Skip. "Maybe I can think better out there."

Neither boy spoke again until they reached the end of the wharf and stood looking out over the harbor. It was a bright morning, and the sea had calmed down again.

"This is where they were standing the first time we saw them," Harvey reminded Skip.

"That's right."

Harvey thrust his hands deep in his pockets and frowned. "Look, Skip, I'm not being stubborn about this just because I'm nosy. That business last night, the way they acted . . . it wasn't right, and you know it."

Skip sighed and sat down on the stringpiece, the heavy squared timber that bordered the edge of the wharf.

"All right. Now what is this business about keeping a watch on Tree House Island?"

Sometimes Harvey's long face seemed to be made of India rubber, so rapidly and completely could it change expression. His frown vanished and a pleased grin took its place as though Skip had thrown a switch. He rubbed his hands together.

"Now you're talking!"

"I ought to have my head examined. But go on."

"Well, the thing I want to know is how often they visit Tree House Island, and at what time, and how long they stay. Now, the best place for us to watch is from the Point."

81

"You mean you want to go out to the Point in the *Fifteen?*"

"No, no. They might see her out there, or Mr. Eph might. Either way would be bad."

"Exactly."

"No, I was thinking we ought to ride our bikes out along Shore Road. We can ditch them in the bushes near Bensons' and walk in through the woods."

The Point was owned by a wealthy Boston family who had their summer home there. They had not come down for the season as yet, but there were sure to be a few workmen around, opening up the big house and getting it ready.

"Of course, that'll mean more trespassing," Skip pointed out. "Maybe that wouldn't matter much any other time, but you and I are in a kind of tender position right now. Can't you imagine what Mr. Eph would say if someone reported we'd been seen prowling around out on the Point and watching Tree House Island with a spyglass?"

"We'll make a wide circle around the house. We'll slip through the woods like Indians," predicted Harv cheerfully. "Once we reach the tip of the Point, nobody will bother us."

"It's a crazy idea. Why should we spend hours out there just to check up on a couple of hole-diggers?" Skip stood up, brushed off the seat of his pants, and sighed again. "Okay, let's go!"

Harvey fetched his bike and telescope and rode up the hill to the parsonage to join Skip. They were about to head for Shore Road when a tremendous racket coming from up the street and around the corner made them pause. A timid stranger might have leaped over the white picket fence in front of the parsonage in an effort to escape the Thing that was approaching, whatever it was. To the boys, however, the sound was familiar.

"Oh-oh, here comes Gumbo."

"Don't say anything about anything. He'll want to tag along."

The sound swelled to a deafening clatter, and then Gumbo came wheeling around the corner in his latest four-wheeled contraption. Made of old wooden boxes, it was low in front

and high in back. It had headlights that worked, a taillight that worked sometimes, a horn that was overworked, and a hand-painted sign on the dashboard that announced "POWER STEERING." The wheels were wooden ones with iron rims. A dragging license plate added to the din as it scraped along behind. The car was Gumbo's latest model — he built a new version about once a week.

He was traveling at quite a clip, but he managed to stop the car by running into the fence and turning over.

"Guess you haven't put in power brakes yet, have you, Gumbo?" said Skip.

"Nope, not yet," said the driver as he crawled nonchalantly out of the wreck. "I didn't expect to want to stop this quick. Hey, how did you guys do last night? I see you got the telescope. Is it all right, Harv?"

"Yes, it's all right."

"I'm sure sorry I left it out there. You had some trip, I guess."

"Oh, you heard, I suppose?"

"Yep. In fact, I was just going down to the harbor to see if you were there."

"As usual, it didn't take the news long to get around," Skip remarked to Harvey.

"I guess not. What else have you heard, Gumbo?"

"I hear Mr. Eph caught you coming in."

Harvey shook his head wonderingly. "Man, this town is something. I suppose everybody's been calling up everybody else."

Gumbo eyed them eagerly.

"Where you guys going?"

"Huh? Why, no place," said Skip, trying to look innocent, but he knew the effort was all but useless. Gumbo was a boy who always seemed to sense when something was doing.

"Hey, lemme get my bike and go along, okay?"

"Now, listen, Gumbo, we're not going anywhere special. Hop aboard that spaceship of yours and beat it, will you?"

84

Gumbo looked from one to the other of the boys, and blew a large bubble of gum that popped like a small explosive charge.

"Well, okay — but if you're not going anywhere special, why can't I come along?"

"Listen, we're just going to ride around. We may not even go any place for a while."

"What you going to do, look at girls through your telescope?" asked Gumbo, and gave a whistle.

"No, we're not going to look at girls. Here, let's see this whingding of yours," said Skip, righting the overturned car. "Say, you're lucky it's still in one piece."

"I guess I better put some kind of brakes on this one," admitted the inventor, inspecting his car.

"I would if I were you. Jump aboard and we'll give you a push up the hill."

"All the way home?" asked Gumbo eagerly.

"Sure." Come on, Harv," said Skip, winking at his pal.

Gumbo wasted no time climbing into the driver's seat. They pushed him home — around the corner and halfway up the block — and left him to consider the problem of installing brakes.

"See you later, Gumbo."

"Okay, guys."

They strolled out of Gumbo's back yard and down to the corner. The instant they were safely out of sight they broke into a run, leaped onto their bicycles, and pedaled for Shore Road as fast as they could. They didn't slow down or speak until they had turned onto it.

85

"Boy! I can just imagine how that squirt would gum up the works if we took him along," said Skip.

"You said it," agreed Harvey.

Shore Road ran along the south side of the harbor and cut across the base of the Point to Wamset Beach. Beach property owners were working on their cottages, getting them ready to rent, but there was not much traffic on the road as yet. Mr. Eph lived high on a hill off Shore Road, too, but fortunately he was safely at the bank at that hour of the day. When the boys neared the entrance to the Benson place, there was no car in sight in either direction.

"All clear?" asked Skip, glancing over his shoulder.

"All clear," said Harvey, watching ahead.

"Okay. Behind those bushes."

Veering off the road they dismounted at a run and rolled their bikes behind a clump of bushes, dropping them in tall grass. They crouched for a moment, peering around, and making sure there were still no cars coming. Then they straightened up and started quietly through the woods, single

86

file, Skip in the lead. Harvey followed with the telescope under his arm.

They soon reached the low stone wall that bounded the Benson property. Scanning the woods ahead, they crossed the wall and picked up a deer trail. Alert to every sound, they padded through the thick tangle of underbrush, bushes, and trees, ready to drop at any instant. They could hear the sound of voices from the direction of the house, but they saw no one. They reached without incident the tip of the Point, where it shelved off steeply to the jumble of rocks below, which even a high tide did not completely cover.

The house sat well back on the highest point of ground. The small hollow they had dropped into shielded them from being seen by anyone there. Screened by low bushes, they lay on their stomachs in the grass. Harvey trained the telescope on Tree House Island.

"See anything?" asked Skip. The air was clear. The island stood out sharply in the sparkling blue waters.

"No sign of them, Skip. Take a look."

Through the telescope the island could be seen in considerable detail. The tiny beach gleamed in the sunshine, a minute, empty patch of sand.

"Check Doane," suggested Harvey.

Skip focused on the larger island.

"I can see the *Leeway* alongside the dock."

"Good. At least we know where they are."

"Maybe they won't come over to Tree House at all."

"Maybe not, but I have a hunch they will. My hunch is it's Tree House Island they're really interested in."

87

"Well, we'll see."

They stretched out and talked for a while in low voices, waiting. They took turns having a look through the telescope from time to time.

Skip was on the point of handing Harvey the telescope when a faint rustling sound made them both start. They froze, and held their breath.

Again they heard the rustling sound, this time closer. The boys exchanged a questioning glance, hopeful that it was only some small animal. But then the sound of human footsteps became unmistakable. They shrank down with their hearts beating fast and with unpleasant pictures of being caught there by some old grouch who would make trouble. Skip turned one eye up fearfully toward the rim of the hollow above their heads. Already he seemed to hear Mr. Eph thundering at them in a voice of doom.

A pair of legs appeared directly above him. Legs that protruded from shorts, and ended in sneakers.

"Hey!" said a voice in a loud whisper. "Skip? Harvey? Where are you?"

The boys sat up, outraged.

"Gumbo! Shut up!" said Skip in an equally loud whisper, and rolled aside as Gumbo leaped like a grasshopper down into the hollow and went head over heels with a crackling and snapping of twigs that would have done justice to a careless buffalo.

"Darn it, what are you doing here?" demanded Harvey. "Want to spoil everything? If they didn't see you from the house we're lucky!"

"What's the big idea, anyway?" Skip demanded furiously.

Gumbo sat up, brushed a few twigs off the back of his neck, and cocked his head sideways in triumph.

"I knew you guys were up to something, so as soon as you left I grabbed my bike and trailed you."

Skip glowered at him. "Might know a pest like you would stick to us like glue."

"He's half bloodhound," grumbled Harvey. "Always has been. Nobody's ever gotten away from him yet. I don't know why we figured *we* could."

"What's going on?" asked Gumbo. "I want to know."

"Nothing's going on!"

"What you looking at through the spyglass? Oh! Tree House Island, I guess, huh? Why?"

"Gumbo, you ask too many questions. What we're doing is none of your business."

"Aw, come on, Skip. I want to know."

"We ought to punch you in the nose, is what we ought to do," growled Skip, and looked so angry that even Gumbo, who had the hide of a rhinoceros, began to get the idea.

"Well, okay, if you're going to be that way, I'll take off," he said, and stood up. "I'm thirsty, I think I'll go up to the house and ask for a drink of water —"

"Sit down!" ordered Skip, and Gumbo was dragged down again. The older boys looked at each other helplessly. "Doggonit, what shall we do?"

Harvey thrust his face close to Gumbo's, as though trying to hypnotize him with his big eyes.

"Gumbo, can you keep a secret?"

"Sure!"

"Would you take an oath in blood?"

Unhesitatingly Gumbo thrust out his arm.

"Try me."

Harvey glanced at Skip.

"I believe this little earwig would actually go through with it. Now, listen, Gumbo. We're only trying to figure out what Dr. Dillingham and Professor Santos are doing out on the island, that's all. But we have to be careful, because after last night we can't afford to get into any more trouble. Especially me."

"We're going to wait here until we see Doc and the professor come over to Tree House Island," added Skip.

"Lemme have a look at the island," said Gumbo, grabbing the telescope.

"Go ahead. And then why don't you sneak back the way you came, because we're probably going to have a long, long wait," said Harvey. "There's no telling how long. This kind of thing calls for a whole lot of patience, and —"

"Hey, those men have a boat with an inboard motor, don't they?" asked Gumbo in a chatty way.

"That's right. Now, let me have the 'scope, Gumbo, and —"

"Wait a minute. One guy's fat and the other guy's little, huh?"

"Yes. Now hand me that —"

"Then that must be them, just coming around the island."

"What?" Harvey grabbed the telescope and looked. "My gosh, he's right!"

"See?" said Gumbo. "I brought you luck."

90

"The day you bring us luck, boy, that will be the day," growled Skip. Harvey passed the telescope on to him. Skip watched while the men dragged the *Leeway* ashore and took several pieces of equipment out of her. The professor carried two shovels up the beach. Doc followed carrying a piece of apparatus that looked like a small posthole digger.

"I'll bet that's what they probe with," said Skip, when Harvey had taken a look.

"Probe for what?" asked Gumbo.

"We don't know. They're probing and digging for something out there, but we don't know what. Doc said it's for worms and insects."

"*Worms?* Why?"

"To see what the birds eat. But we think they're digging for something else."

"What?"

Harvey paused in his study of the island to shoot a lofty stare at Gumbo.

"Listen, squirt, if we knew that we wouldn't be here." He resumed his looking. "I think they're getting set to dig again."

The boys took turns watching, but were able to catch only occasional glimpses of the men on the island.

"Well, I'm hungry," said Harvey presently. "I guess we've seen all there is to see. What say we head for home?"

Skip got the idea. They would go home, ditch Gumbo, and return again later on. He yawned and stretched.

"Okay, let's go. But be quiet."

Cautiously the three boys left their hiding-place and started back through the woods. Skip took the lead, and Harvey brought up the rear, with Gumbo in the middle where they could keep an eye on him.

All went well until Gumbo stumbled over a dead limb that had fallen across the trail. It snapped with a crack that seemed louder than a pistol shot.

"Darn!" he exclaimed.

"Hey! Who's that over there in the woods?" they heard a deep voice ask. It was one of the workmen, close by, on the other side of some thick underbrush.

"Maybe it's a deer," said another man.

"Deer don't say 'Darn!'" snorted the first man, and the boys heard heavy footsteps tramping their way.

Fortunately, Gumbo had been in so much hot water in his time, one way or another, that he reacted quickly to it.

"Get down!" he whispered, and darted on ahead, making as much noise as he could.

"Hey there!" called the deep voice. Gumbo stopped.

"Hi!" he said in an innocent chirp. "I was chasing a baby rabbit. Almost caught him, too."

The deep voice laughed. "Shucks, it's Gumbo Phillips. What are you doing out here, Gumbo?"

"Hi, Mr. Feeney." It was a man they all knew. "Oh, I was just fooling around."

"Well, fool around somewhere else. This here's private property, and the Bensons don't want you kids tramping around in here."

"Okay, Mr. Feeney. So long," said Gumbo, and went whistling on his way.

7

WHEN THE BOYS reached their bikes, Gumbo was sitting cross-legged beside them, playing mumblety-peg while he waited. He looked up and grinned as they appeared.

"Hey, that was a close one, guys!"

"Gumbo, I guess we'll have to make you a member of the club," said Skip. "That was all right."

"Of course, you should have picked up your big feet in the first place," remarked Harvey, rapping Gumbo's crown with his knuckles. "Ow! Boy, have you got a hard head! But anyway, hard or not, you certainly used it, which is something."

"This is just between the three of us, though, Gumbo," said Skip. "You've got to promise you won't say anything about what we're doing to anybody."

"You think Doc and the professor are digging for buried treasure or something out there?" asked Gumbo, looking eagerly at Harvey. "Maybe real pieces of eight this time?"

"No, nothing like that."

"We don't know what they're after," said Skip. "We're just wondering. But anyway, keep it under your hat."

"Don't worry, I will," said Gumbo, and the boys felt certain that there, at least, they could count on him.

"Okay. Now, you can be our scout," said Skip. "Go ahead out onto the road, and give us the high sign if the coast is clear."

Gumbo picked up his bike, scouted the road, and waved them out of hiding. They pedaled away along Shore Road and were soon back in Goose Harbor. Before they split up for lunch, Gumbo said, "When are you going out to watch again?"

"Well, I want to check my boat first and see what's doing down at the harbor," said Skip, "so I don't know."

Harvey had an idea.

"Listen, Gumbo, how about you taking the telescope and going out there this afternoon to check up for us?"

But Gumbo wasn't sure he wanted to go alone.

"What's the matter?" asked Harvey. "Afraid?"

"Course not! But what's the fun of going alone?"

"Now, look, if you're going to be in on this and help us, you can't expect it all to be fun."

Gumbo finally agreed to take the first watch that afternoon.

"But only if I get to go again when you guys go!"

After lunch Skip and Harvey met at the harbor and rowed out to the *Fifteen* to bail her dry. The rain had continued for some time after they had gotten in the night before.

While they were at the mooring, a boat entered the harbor. They stopped bailing and watched her come.

94

"Well, what do you know? They've knocked off for a while."

"Let's go ashore and be on the wharf to say hello, Skip."

"Feeling sociable?"

"I want to have a look at them. Never know what we might learn."

"Okay, Sherlock, let's go."

They were sitting on the wharf when the *Leeway* came alongside the float. Doc was his usual smiling, waving self, but he looked tired and his smile did not seem to switch on quite as easily as usual. Dark circles of sweat under the arms of his tent-sized shirt indicated he had been getting plenty of exercise. He was wearing an old Panama hat, and as he stepped onto the float he took it off to mop his face with an enormous white handkerchief.

"Well, lads. We meet again."

"Hi, Doc. Hi, Professor," said Skip. Professor Santos rolled his eyes their way and gave them a short nod as he made the boat fast. Doc came up the ladder slowly, holding on in a gingerly way with the tips of his fingers.

"How's it going?" asked Harvey.

Doc paused at the top of the ladder and a hint of peevishness slipped through the smiling mask for an instant, as though the question goaded him. But then he managed his rich, throaty chuckle.

"Believe me, lads, there are easier ways to make a living. Science can be a hard taskmaster."

Lines of weariness were etched in the pouches under his small eyes, and he slouched forward as he walked away up the wharf. Professor Santos followed quickly. Small and compact, he gave the impression of being as tireless as a steel spring.

As the boys watched, a new development caught their attention. The door of Lee Rand's shop opened, and out came a person they had never expected to see there.

"Well, look at that!" exclaimed Skip.

"What do you suppose he came to see Lee about?"

"Nothing pleasant, I'll bet."

Noticing the two ornithologists coming up the wharf, Mr. Eph turned and greeted them with one of his rare smiles.

"Well, gentlemen, good afternoon. How is your work going out on the islands? Well, I hope?"

"We're making progress, Mr. Fairchild, making progress,"

Doc assured him, and held up his palms as the old gentleman offered his hand. "Excuse me for not shaking hands, but I'm in rather bad shape."

"By Joe, you've got some nasty blisters there," declared Mr. Eph. "How did you do that?"

"Well, you wouldn't think an ornithologist would have to go in much for spadework, but that's what we're doing. We're particularly interested in what portion of the insect food available to birds on the islands comes from the soil. You can't be an ornithologist without being an entomologist as well, not to mention an ecologist, you know, sir."

"I can well appreciate that," said Mr. Eph. "Is there anything our club could do to help?"

"Not at the moment, Mr. Fairchild, but perhaps later on. And many thanks to all of you for your interest. Right now I want to get something for these hands, and then hurry back to make a further check on those black-crowned night herons nesting at the far end of the larger island. It's very interesting how they . . ."

The three men walked up toward Front Street, chatting, and disappeared around the corner. Skip turned to Harvey.

"Well, how do you like that? Mr. Eph in Lee's shop."

"Let's go ask Lee what he was doing there."

They found the artist standing in the middle of the shop frowning blackly, filling the small room with smoke as he puffed angrily on his pipe.

"What's the matter, Lee?"

"Mr. Eph been giving you trouble?"

97

Lee's deep-set eyes flashed, and his jaw tightened until the pipestem was in danger of finding itself in two pieces. His hair seemed almost to bristle, as though Mr. Eph had made it stand up.

"He's going to give me trouble, all right, if . . ."

"If what?"

"Oh, the same old thing. He's afraid Mary's getting serious about me, and he doesn't want that."

"Well, so what? What can he do about it?"

"Plenty. He can make life miserable for both of us. Believe it or not, he could make Mary leave Goose Harbor and go home."

"How?"

"If he said she wasn't welcome to stay in his house any more, she wouldn't have any place to go, because nobody else in town would dare take her in. For one thing, nobody would want to interfere in a family quarrel, and in the second place they'd be too scared of Mr. Eph. And then — as he was explaining to me in words of one syllable just now — he could also give me a hard time. The bank owns this building, you know. So the bank could find a number of pretexts for putting me out, if he wanted it to."

"You mean he was threatening to put you out of here if you don't stop seeing Mary?"

"That's what it amounted to."

"Well, if you ask me, that's just plain dirty," declared Skip angrily. "He tries to run everybody's life!"

Lee sent up a few more smoke signals that looked like war clouds, but then he sighed and his shoulders sagged.

"Well, I hardly know what to do," he admitted. "He holds so many of the cards."

The shop's screen door flew open with a violence that made the shop bell clank like a cowbell. Mary Fairchild had entered.

"Well!" She planted herself before them with her hands on her hips and stared at Lee with the light of battle in her eyes. "Was my grandfather just here to see you, Lee?"

"Yes."

Skip nudged Harvey.

"Hi, Mary. So long, Lee, we've got to get moving."

The fire faded momentarily in Mary's eyes as she gave them a grateful look.

"Thanks, fellows. We'll see you later."

"Sure."

They slipped out of the shop and left Mary and Lee to their private problems.

"Doggonit, I don't understand what Mr. Eph sees wrong with Lee, anyway," complained Skip as they walked away. "Just because he isn't a stockbroker or something, I suppose old Moneybags thinks he isn't good enough for her."

"Mr. Eph's like a lot of people, he thinks all artists are crazy, or no good. Just because of a few guys like Ferdy Gotz and Emil Belden," said Harvey, mentioning two members of Goose Harbor's art colony who were more noted for their drinking parties than their paintings.

They were walking toward the Sou'wester Inn to fetch their bikes when Gumbo came racing along Front Street and hailed them.

99

"Hey, guys!" He skidded to a stop and leaped off his bike, his eyes round with news. "Hey, guess what! They left the island and headed for —"

"Look out!" Harvey grabbed Gumbo's bike and jerked it to the curb. "Get out of the street before you get hit!"

Across the street, Doc and the professor had just come out of Nickerson's Drugstore. Doc seemed to hesitate for a fraction of a second, but it was impossible to be sure whether or not he had heard Gumbo.

In the meantime Gumbo was looking up and down the street, and the only thing that happened to be moving at the moment was old Miss Gurnet, who was crossing at the corner. The only cars in sight were all parked.

"Whatcha mean? Who's going to hit me?"

"I am, if you don't shut your trap," muttered Harvey fiercely, while Skip was waving and saying "Hi" to the men. Having warned Gumbo, Harvey mustered up a bright smile and spoke to the men, too.

Doc's smile wreathed his round face benevolently while his small eyes narrowed. Perhaps it could have been the bright sunlight that made them react, perhaps not.

"How's it going?"

"Fine, Doc."

"Good. See you later, lads," he said, and waddled off down the street, raising his hat to Miss Gurnet as she approached. By this time Gumbo was staring at the men openmouthed.

Skip grabbed his wrist and yanked him around.

"Stop staring at them, dopey," he muttered. "Doggonit, we ought to clobber you."

"How did I know they were going to walk out of the drugstore?" squawked Gumbo. "Gee whiz!"

"Well, when you've got something to tell us, don't tell it right in the middle of Front Street, for Pete's sake!"

"Okay, Harv, okay!"

"I wonder if Doc heard," muttered Harvey worriedly, as they walked on toward the inn, with Gumbo wheeling his bike beside them. Harvey was deep in thought for a moment. Then he shook his head slowly. "Well, anyway, I can tell you one thing. From now on, we've got to be extra careful!"

By threatening Gumbo within an inch of his life, the boys were able to make him promise to stay home when they went back out to the Point at dusk that evening.

"You'd have to be home by nine-thirty, anyway, and we'll stay a lot later than that," said Skip.

"All right for you guys!" said Gumbo in an aggrieved tone of voice.

It was pretty certain that all the workmen at the Benson place had long since left for the day, but even so the boys took all the same precautions they had taken the first time, moving through the woods as silently as possible and staying on the lookout for trouble.

The woods were nearly dark now. The deer trail was but a dim line through the gloom. A rabbit bounded away into the underbrush ahead of them, and once they flushed a pheasant that disappeared in a long glide through a break in the trees.

By the time they reached the hollow on the tip of the Point, the haze of dusk had softened Tree House Island's outlines

101

and dimmed its colors. Further out, Doane Island was a dark patch on the water.

There was no sign of the *Leeway* out at Tree House Island.

"We're probably wasting our time coming here now," said Skip, after they had each had a look through the telescope. "They probably won't bother to go tonight. I don't imagine Doc will want to do any more digging with those hands."

"Maybe not. But still, the only way we can be sure is to be here and watch for a while."

"That's right. Well, anyway, we've got a nice night for it."

They waited as patiently as they could for over an hour. Low in the east, the great triangle of Deneb, Altair, and Vega appeared. Gradually the other stars filled in. A lopsided moon rose, adding its light to the scene. The boys whiled the time away by talking about some of the girls who would soon be coming to their family cottages for the summer. In general, they found themselves pretty much in agreement as to which ones were creeps and which ones were okay. It was an interesting enough discussion, but it was hard to give the proper concentration to such matters when they had the men and the islands on their minds.

They were considering calling it a night when Skip, taking a check with the telescope, picked up a sign of movement on the water.

"Hey. I see a boat."

"Coming toward the island?"

"Yes."

"From the right direction?"

"Yes. It must be them."

Harvey took a look.

"Sure. They're putting in to the cove now."

They waited. Dimly they could see specks of light move up the beach toward the center of the island.

"Look at that, Skip. I'll bet they're going to dig some more after all."

"It must be pretty important, whatever they're doing. They're putting in some mighty long hours of hard back-breaking work, Harv. Doc looked about done in this afternoon."

"He sure did. It's all pretty strange. And what bothers me is, all we can do is sit here and watch. I don't know what they're doing, but for all we know they may finish up and leave any time, and then maybe we'll all find out something after it's too late."

Skip stared out over the moonlit water at the island, wondering how to get at its secret.

"I wish there was someone we dared talk to about all this,"

he remarked. "I'd like to see what someone else would think — someone who would take us seriously."

"So would I," agreed Harvey.

He cracked a knuckle with a thoughtful air. Then he turned to Skip.

"Say! Maybe there *is* someone."

"Who?"

"Lee."

"Lee Rand?"

"Why not?"

Skip considered. "Say, maybe you're right. He'd at least listen with an open mind. And anything we said wouldn't go any farther, either."

Harvey took one last look at the island, and pushed the telescope together.

"Well, we know they're out there again, and I think we've learned about all we can from this distance. What say we go back to town? I'm for talking to Lee if you are."

"Let's go."

When they reached the wharf they found Lee's shop dark.

"I'll bet he's out with Mary somewhere."

"Probably. I wonder what they decided to do about Mr. Eph."

"I wonder. Well, how about seeing him first thing in the morning?"

"Okay. Come down to the inn as soon as you can," said Harvey, and they parted for the night.

8

THEY REACHED THE WHARF a few minutes after eight. It was a brisk, cool morning, with a stiff onshore breeze rippling the bay. Lee was sitting in his second-floor studio window holding a mug of steaming coffee and looking out moodily at the harbor. He was obviously a man with a lot on his mind.

"Hi, Lee," they called.

He lifted the coffee mug in a listless salute.

"Hi, Lee, hi, Lo," he said. "Lee is low this morning, fellows. Feelin' mighty low."

"Girl trouble?"

"Girl trouble, and grandpa trouble. I don't know which is worse."

"Can we come up and talk to you for a minute?"

"No. Go away and let me suffer."

"Well . . ." The boys looked at each other, nonplussed. Skip raised his eyebrows in a silent question, and Harvey shrugged. Much as they felt the need of advice, it looked as if they would have to go somewhere else. Where else they might go was not apparent to them at the moment, but nevertheless Skip glanced up and said, "Okay, Lee. We'll see you later."

They started to turn away, when Lee spoke again.

"Wait a minute. Something special on your minds?"

"Yes."

"Something that can't wait?"

"Well . . . not very well, it can't," Skip admitted.

"Well, then, come on up. The shop door's open."

They went inside and climbed the tight spiral staircase to the studio.

"I shouldn't spend my time sitting around here feeling sorry for myself, anyway," declared Lee. "Sit down and tell me *your* problems. Pour yourself some coffee first."

They fitted themselves out with mugs of coffee and sat down in a couple of canvas chairs.

"Okay, what's the pitch, fellows?" asked Lee.

Skip exchanged a glance with Harvey, and cleared his throat.

"Lee, something's going on that we can't quite figure out, and it's something we can't talk to just anybody about, so we decided to come talk to you."

"I'm flattered," said Lee, not without a touch of irony. "Us outcasts have to band together."

"That's about what it comes to," Harvey put in. "We *are* sort of outcasts, as far as this particular matter is concerned. We've almost gotten into a mess of trouble over it already."

"Oh? This is something about that pair out on Doane Island, eh?"

"Gee, have you heard about that, too?"

"Sure. When you left the meeting you went out to Tree House Island to get your telescope. Mr. Eph got wind of it, and you had to see him at the bank. Sure I heard. The jungle drums were beating out the news all over town before you'd hardly reached the bank."

"The good old bush telegraph," said Harvey. "No small town should be without one."

"No small town *is* without one," said Lee. "But go on, Skip. What about those guys on the island?"

Skip started the story, and Harvey cut in from time to time. Between them, they told Lee the whole thing, from the moment the smiling fat man and the small dark man first appeared on the wharf to the moment, in the dark on the Point, when they decided to talk to him about them.

Lee listened almost without an interruption. When they had finished he looked from one boy to the other, and burst out laughing.

"Well, I can see your problem, all right. The whole thing does sound like exactly the sort of story people have learned to expect from Harvey Harding."

The boys were keenly disappointed by his laughter. Was he going to scoff at their suspicions and dismiss them as ridiculous?

"All of Goose Harbor's decent, law-abiding citizens from Ephraim Fairchild on down are charmed with the distinguished visiting scientists, and you want to stir up trouble," Lee went on. "Yes, I can see your problem. And so you came to me. With a sure instinct, you picked the only person who . . ."

Shaking his head wonderingly, he rose and crossed the tiny room to a pile of drawings on a table. He pawed through them and picked out a sketch pad. While the boys watched silently, Lee sat down, opened the pad, and studied some sketches for a long while.

"Sketches I made of Doc Dillingham at the Birdbrains' meeting," he declared, and held them up. Both boys rose and took a close look.

"They're sure good, Lee," said Skip. "Real good."

"They look like Doc the way *I* see him," remarked Harvey.

Lee gave him an interested glance. Then he continued to study the drawings. The boys sat down and waited. The

artist seemed to be turning a great many things over in his mind.

"An interesting face," he remarked at last. "An unusual face. A smiling mask of a face . . . with deadly eyes."

The unexpected and exciting words made Harvey spill coffee down the front of his tee shirt. He sat forward plucking his shirt away from his scalded chest and waving the wet spot in the breeze.

"Say! Do you see it that way, too, Lee?"

"Yes."

"And what about Professor Santos?"

"One step from the jungle. He'd take great delight in shrinking your heads down to the size of your fist."

"Lee, you're right on the button, or I'm crazy!" cried Harvey. "You should have seen him that night out on Tree House Island, when he was mad."

"This is great!" said Skip. "You mean to say you already had your own suspicions about them, Lee?"

The artist considered for a space of three puffs on his pipe. "Well, let's put it this way. I felt they were men concerning whom nothing would surprise me."

His eyes goggling behind his thick glasses, Harvey rose and began to blunder around the room as his mind commenced to function at high speed.

"Sit down, Harv, before you wreck the joint," said Skip, and Harvey sat down. But he was ready and eager now to move ahead.

"All right. So now we're at least agreed that Doc and the professor look like they could be more than a pair of harmless

109

ornithologists," he said. "Now the next step is to decide what it is they could be doing out there. What could they be digging for that's so important?"

Skip laughed. "Gumbo was all ready to settle for pieces of eight again," he remarked. "Buried treasure."

Lee glanced at him oddly, and sipped his coffee.

"Well, now," he said, "for that matter, let's stop and analyze what it is people usually dig for. The only thing they usually dig for very energetically, day and night, is something valuable, isn't it? In other words, some kind of buried treasure?"

"You're taking the words right out of my mouth, Lee," declared Harvey happily. "Skip, I've never said so until now, but that's exactly the line of reasoning that's occurred to me. The only question is, what could be out there that's valuable?"

They all looked at each other for a moment. Skip grinned. "Uranium?"

"No, I don't think Tree House Island is a likely place for high-grade ore," said Harvey — regretfully, to be sure. "And I don't think any pirates ever buried their gold there."

"Not pirates, no," Lee agreed in a thoughtful murmur, "and not gold . . ."

There was something about Lee's inward-turning, memory-searching expression as he stared out the window with blank eyes that made Skip sit forward and ask an eager question.

"Something else, you mean?"

Lee glanced around at them, and pulled at his lower lip. "Maybe."

110

Then he moved his head impatiently, as if shaking off the idea, and rose to refill his coffee mug.

"It's probably crazy, crazy as can be. But still it's the only thing I can think of that has any possibility of fitting the situation, so we might as well explore it, if only for kicks." He poured, and then sat down again. "You fellows have heard of the big bank robbery over in Lanfield about twenty years ago, haven't you?"

"Sure. I've heard it mentioned lots of times," said Skip.

"Uncle Nate told me about it once. He knew the man in Gorgon Bay who saw one of the robbers —"

Lee held up his hand.

"Hold that for now, Harv. I want to give you the story straight through from the beginning, as I knew it, because I grew up with it and spent hours on end working out different theories about it. I used to lie awake nights sometimes, thinking up angles.

"I was eight when the bank was robbed, and I grew up in Lanfield, you know, so I heard plenty about it. For years afterwards it was a standard topic of conversation. Why, it was a year or more before some of our local optimists along the coast here gave up hope that somehow some of the loot would finally wash ashore, still intact.

"Well, of course, we Lanfield kids never played cowboys and Indians after that. With us it was always cops and bank robbers. And the whole incident fascinated me even more than it did most kids. When I grew older I even went down and pestered the editor of the *Courier* into letting me see their clippings file. I read everything they had about it. And

111

all these years, a lot of unanswered questions have stayed in the back of my mind. . . . More coffee, fellows?"

"I'll get it," said Harvey, hopping up. "Just go on."

"No, I'll get it," said Skip, beating him to it. "I don't want you pouring my coffee at a time like this, Harv," he told his absent-minded friend. "You'd probably pour it in my lap."

"Okay, okay," said Harvey, impatient at the interruption. "Go ahead, Lee."

"Well, now, about the bank robbery. On the sixteenth of September in 1938, two masked men jumped out of a car, rushed into the Lanfield First National Bank, and slugged the guard before he could even get out his gun. They herded everybody in the bank together, and filled up two sacks they were carrying. Money for the shoe factory payroll had just been brought to the bank — they'd obviously planned on that — so they made a good haul."

"How much was it they got in all?"

"One hundred and six thousand dollars, all in cash."

The boys whistled, paying an appropriate tribute to the sum.

"Meanwhile the guard came to. He was groggy, but as they started to leave he managed to drag out his gun and get off a shot from the floor. One of the robbers — people in the bank afterwards described him as tall, thin, and soft-spoken — whirled and fired twice. He killed the guard.

"They rushed out, jumped in the car — a third man was waiting at the wheel — and took off.

"Well, of course word went out right away to all police,

112

and roadblocks were soon thrown up on all roads leading out of Lanfield. There was great excitement, every car was stopped, lots of old ladies fainted, and so on, but no sign of the robbers.

"That night, up off Gorgon Bay, they had a violent squall. A couple of men were down on the beach, trying to get some flash pictures of the breakers, when they saw what looked like a body in the surf. Before they could even reach him, however, the swimmer showed signs of life and managed to stumble ashore under his own power. They helped him up onto the beach, and the guy with the camera took a flash picture of him which later appeared in newspapers from coast to coast for reasons the photographer never dreamed of when he snapped it. Weak as he was, the rescued man protested about the picture, but he couldn't do anything about it.

"The photographer ran up to a beach cottage for a bottle of liquor to give the guy a drink. Meanwhile, after resting for a few minutes, the stranger was getting his breath back and looking pretty good. He told the other man there'd been two others in the boat with him, and asked him to go back down to the water's edge and look for them.

"By the time the two rescuers returned, the one with a bottle and the other from the water's edge, the rescued man had vanished. They never saw him again.

"Well, the photographer developed his picture, and it was a beaut. Very dramatic rescue picture. Also, of course, it was intriguing. Who was the man in the picture?

"At first the picture was only printed locally. And the

minute it came out, the police began to get calls. Several people here in Goose Harbor recognized the man as one of three fishermen who had kept a boat in the harbor for the past few weeks and turned up regularly in an old Model T Ford to go fishing. Someone in Gorgon Bay recognized him as a man who had rented a beach cottage there a couple of days earlier and left a car parked alongside it. By then, of course, the car was gone.

"Naturally, the story and the picture were picked up by one of the wire services and sent all over the country. Meanwhile the police had made some progress themselves. They had found the getaway car in an old barn on a summer place near Lanfield which the same man had also rented — again, the owner recognized him from the picture. Then the Chicago police came through with a real clue. The man in the photo looked very much like a small-time Chicago con man named Skinny Arnold. Arnold, it seemed, was an unusual crook. He appeared to be smarter than average, and to have big ideas which he had never, as yet, put into operation. The police had never been able to book him on any but minor charges, and had never managed to convict him of anything.

"His rogues' gallery pictures were published in the papers alongside the famous photograph, and everybody agreed it was the same man. The hunt was on, but no trace of him was ever found. One rumor was that he slipped into Canada and escaped from there to South America on a tramp steamer, but nothing was ever proved.

"Going back to the robbery, now, all the pieces gradually began to fit together. This Arnold was a smooth operator who

114

believed in using psychology, and the plan he worked out was something like this:

"He knew that as soon as the alarm was given after the robbery, all roads leading away from Lanfield would have roadblocks thrown across them, and all the police would be expecting him and his pals to make a break inland in their high-powered car. So instead of driving toward the roadblocks in a high-powered car, they drove *away* from them in an old Model T Ford. Three men in old fishing clothes, puttering down to Goose Harbor in an old Model T Ford loaded with fishing tackle! Who would ever suspect them of anything? Besides, people had seen them there often, going out fishing.

"So they raced away from the bank and drove out in the country to the barn, which was off in the woods down a secluded side road. There they changed clothes and cars. They made the rest of their getaway at about ten miles an hour — and probably more than one police car raced past them along the way. I imagine a couple of their tackle boxes were loaded with the loot.

"At the harbor they put their gear in their boat and started out for all the world like three guys out to do some fishing and maybe put in along the beach somewhere for overnight, to spend the evening and early morning surf-casting.

"The next thing known about their whereabouts is eight hours later, when Arnold crawled ashore at Gorgon Bay. A few days after that the bodies of the other two turned up. One couldn't be identified — not enough left of him. The other was finally identified as a man known to the police in Los Angeles."

115

Skip sipped his coffee, and found it had grown stone-cold.

"Golly! I never heard the whole story before," he said. "That's quite a yarn."

"Yes, but now we come to the important part," said Lee. "The money. What happened to the money?"

"Went down with the boat, I suppose."

"Well, naturally, that's what people assumed at the time, and maybe that's what did happen," said Lee. "However, that money is the only treasure I can think of connected with this neck of the woods which, if it still *did* exist, would be juicy enough to make a couple of men like Doc and Professor Santos go digging for it."

"Say!" Harvey was on his feet again, and completely in his element. "You mean you think it might be buried out on Tree House Island, and that Doc and the professor somehow got wind of the fact? Met Skinny Arnold down in South America, maybe?"

Lee nodded.

"Something like that. Just for the sake of argument, now, let's assume that the money *is* buried out there. Next, then, the question is — how did it get there?"

Harvey's mind was racing ahead by leaps and bounds now.

"It was part of the robbers' plan from the start!" he suggested. "Hide the dough somewhere as soon as possible — get it out of their possession so's they wouldn't be caught with it — and come back for it later when the heat was off!"

Again Lee nodded. "Well, at least that fits in with the rest of Arnold's psychological approach. If I'm right about him,

116

he always tried to do the opposite of what anyone might expect — and who would expect bank robbers to escape in a small boat and bury their loot on an island? They could bury the money, then go on to Gorgon Bay and take off in the car they had left there. Then, even if they were stopped somewhere, they wouldn't be caught with the money. Even if they were caught and had to do time, the money would be there waiting for them when they finally got out. Of course, the murder changed that picture, but not enough to make them alter their carefully set up plan."

For a moment they were all silent as they mulled over this incredible but fascinating theory.

"It's strange, but the minute you mentioned digging on the island, that whole bank robbery business popped up in my mind. I haven't given it a thought for years now, either. . . . Well, it may be crazy, but it's still the best possible reason I can think of for two strangers to be out on Tree House Island digging like madmen," said Lee. "And after all, if it hadn't been for Arnold getting caught in that squall and capsizing, and then having that guy take his picture when he came ashore, a plan like that might have worked like a dream. It was the picture that spoiled everything."

Lee stood up and put his coffee mug aside.

"And then, of course, five days later, on the twenty-first of September, the big hurricane of '38 struck the coast, and that little island was nearly blown off the map. It would be hard to go out there now and find something you'd buried twenty years ago, what with nearly all the big trees gone . . ."

117

He turned to the boys with the air of a man who had committed himself to see something through, even at the risk of feeling foolish later on.

"How would you fellows like to take a run over to Lanfield?" he asked. "I think I'll ask Jed Bodfish — he's the editor of the *Courier* — to let me see those old clippings just once more."

9

LEE DUG HIS CAR KEYS out of a pair of trousers in the closet and followed the boys down the spiral staircase. At the door, Harvey held up his hand. He could not help being dramatic at a time like this. Everything in him that made him an actor and playwright went into a gesture worthy of a conspirator in an Italian opera as he halted his friends.

"Wait a minute!"

"What's the matter?"

He peeped out cautiously.

"Let's try to get out of here without being seen."

"Who are you worrying about? Doc?" asked Skip.

"No."

"Mr. Eph?"

"No. Gumbo! If that squirt sees us we'll never shake him off."

Skip laughed. "Oh, come on, Harv, let's take a chance. We can't be unlucky every time."

They crossed the wharf and went through a passageway into Abernathy's Boatyard, where Lee had his old beach wagon parked. A few minutes later they were leaving Goose Harbor on the road to Lanfield.

"I'm almost disappointed," declared Skip. "Gumbo's slipping."

Lanfield was twelve miles west-northwest of Goose Harbor. It was the county seat, and the largest town in the county, with a population of seventeen thousand. Its weekly newspaper covered the whole county, with correspondents in all towns.

"Be nice to see Jed Bodfish again," said Lee. "He's a nice old guy. He'll probably kid me when I come in again after all these years with the same old request."

"I wonder what he'd say if we told him what was on our minds?" said Harvey.

"I hate to think," said Lee, "especially with you in our party. That was quite a story the *Courier* did about your pieces-of-eight rumor, by the way."

"Very funny," said Harvey with a sour look that sent his friends into fits of laughter.

"I might as well warn you, Harv, you'll probably come in for some kidding from old Jed yourself when he finds out who you are."

Harvey's face lengthened with a martyred look that showed he didn't relish the prospect.

"I'm a little tired of hearing about those pieces of eight," he admitted.

Lee laughed again, a laugh that ended in a sigh.

"Well, whatever we find out or don't find, I've got to admit this beats sitting around in the studio moping all day," he declared. He glanced at the boys solemnly. "Take my advice, fellows. Never get mixed up seriously with a girl. What a headache they can be!"

"Well, I'll tell you one thing, I don't envy you right now, Lee," said Skip. "The last time we saw Mary, she sure had fire in her eyes."

"And where there was fire there was smoke, too, my boy. Trouble is, she's a real Fairchild herself. She's so mad she wants to run off and get married and then come back to Goose Harbor and roost in the studio and defy her grandpa to put the two of us out."

Harvey clapped his bony hands together and rubbed them approvingly.

"Say, I'm in favor of that!" he declared. "Man, would that stand Goose Harbor on its ear! And everyone would love it, too."

"Sounds like the makings of a Harvey Harding play," remarked Skip. "Couldn't be a better situation if you dreamed it up yourself."

"That's right," agreed Lee. "Sometimes I think Mary ought to collaborate with him on a couple of plays. What those two could turn out!"

"Well, at any rate, I guess you didn't go for her idea," said Skip.

"Listen, I'd like to get married, too, but I don't want to do it that way. When we get married I want to do it right. I want to march into the church and stand up in front of your dad with everybody there, including Grandpa, and I want to look him in the eye when I do it."

"And what did Mary say to that?"

"She said it's impossible. She's a very impulsive girl, and an impatient one, too. So we went round and round, and . . . well, it was a very wearing evening."

"I'll bet."

"What are you going to do about it all?" asked Harvey, always interested in resolving the plot.

"As of this moment," said Lee, "I don't know."

The *Courier* had a neat new building, in keeping with the times, but it was in front of an old-fashioned roll-top desk, sitting in an ancient swivel chair, that they found its venerable editor.

Mr. Bodfish was looking over a galley proof as the visitors approached. He shot a sideways glance at them, and then swung around from his desk and tipped his steel-rimmed glasses onto his forehead. He was a spare old man with shrewd, kindly eyes and a stubborn jaw. He was of Ephraim

122

Fairchild's generation, and very much like him in many ways. In fact, they were two old pieces of flint that had managed to strike a lot of sparks off one another through the years. The Goose Harbor Cooperative Bank had been advertising in the Lanfield *Courier* for half a century. Eph Fairchild got mad about something in the paper on an average of once every other week. Each time his anger led swiftly to a hot session on the telephone with Jed Bodfish, in which he roared insults at Jed and canceled the bank's weekly ad. Jed roared insults back, and ran the ad anyway. And the following week Eph paid the bill for it as usual.

The old editor made them welcome with a broad smile as he recognized a home-town boy.

"Well, if it isn't Lee Rand! By George, you're pretty near grown now, aren't you?"

"Yes, I've shot right up," grinned Lee, as they shook hands. "Haven't changed much, though. I'm back on the same old errand."

"What? Still working on the bank robbery?"

"Yes, sir."

Lee introduced the two boys. He limited the introduction to the bare mention of their names, but the editor was not one who missed recognizing a name that had been in the news. Harvey fidgeted uncomfortably as the shrewd old eyes twinkled in his direction.

"Harvey Harding, eh? Well, well! Isn't every day we have a celebrity come into the office," he declared. "Harvey, I want to thank you for a peach of a story. I was especially grateful for the part about Eph Fairchild being caught with a rake in

123

his jeep. He nearly melted twelve miles of telephone wire when he phoned me about that bit."

The old man had a hearty laugh at the memory of that enjoyable conversation, and then turned his attention back to Lee.

"Well, did you put those clippings back in their proper place last time you looked at them?"

"Of course. Think I wanted to get skinned alive?"

"All right, then, I guess you can look at 'em again. We've got a special room for our files now — very fancy we're getting to be around here. Second door down. Help yourself, Lee."

They thanked him and went down the hall to the files.

"New filing cabinets, and everything. Some class," said Lee. He ran his eyes down the drawers, and opened one. "This ought to do it. . . . Ah! New cabinets, maybe, but the same old folder," he commented as he brought out a fat Manila envelope.

They sat down with it around a table in a corner of the room. In the envelope were clippings from a great many sources, not only the *Courier* but other papers. Lee spread out the yellowed clippings and together they read about the event that had shocked Lanfield twenty years ago.

"I knew the bank guard that was killed," remarked Lee. "He was a nice old fellow. Gus Willard was his name. He was the kind that took the trouble to notice us kids. Used to stick his thumbs in his gun belt and rock back and forth on his heels whenever one of us said hello. He knew we were get-

124

ting a kick out of looking at his gun. I guess he never thought he'd die trying to use it."

Among the clippings were two or three reproductions of the famous photograph. The boys studied the faded cuts eagerly.

"So that's him!"

"That's him. But now, I want to take a look in the photo files and see if I can find a glossy print of the picture."

Lee returned to the filing cabinets and rooted around in them for a while, but with no success.

"Darn. That's really what I was especially interested in seeing. These old clippings aren't clear enough to be much help."

He stood frowning at the cabinets for a moment, disappointed. But the Brain had not been idle, and neither had the big brown eyes behind the thick glasses.

"What about all those photos over Mr. Bodfish's desk? I noticed the third one from the right looked like it might be the picture you told us about, and now that I see these I'm sure it was."

"Say, I'll bet you're right. Those are his favorite news photos of the past — it certainly must be among them. Come on, let's go see," said Lee, and then pulled up short. "Oh, wait a minute. First let me put these clippings back."

He returned the clippings to their folder, restored the folder to the files, and then led the way back to Mr. Bodfish's desk.

"Find what you wanted?" asked the old editor.

"Yes, thanks. Everything but a glossy of the Arnold photo,

and I'm hoping you've got one here — yes, sir, third from the right," said Lee, pointing out the photo and glancing at Harvey with an admiring chuckle. "You ought to take this kid on as a reporter, Mr. Bodfish. He never misses a thing."

"That so? H'm." The editor looked him up and down. "Maybe we ought to have a talk sometime, when he's a little older," he declared, but the whole conversation was lost on Harvey. He was absorbed in an eager study of the photo. The others joined him in contemplating the dramatic picture of the dripping, exhausted man being helped up the beach.

Mr. Bodfish sighed, and shook his head in a ruminative way.

"I'd give a lot to know whatever became of that fellow," he declared.

Lee leaned closer to the photo. If the smoke his pipe was creating was any clue to his emotions, he was breathing hard.

Mr. Bodfish picked up a sheaf of galley proofs.

"Well, got to run out to the composing room for a few minutes. Come in again, Lee. Glad to have met you, boys."

They all shook hands, and Mr. Bodfish left the office. Lee glanced after him over his shoulder.

"That's a break. Got to be careful here. I wouldn't want him to get wind of anything, but I did want a chance to be alone with this photo for a minute."

"Why? What's on your mind, Lee?"

His outward calm failed to conceal the fact that Lee was intensely excited. His excitement tingled contagiously in the air of the small room as he opened the sketchbook he had been carrying under his arm. Only then did the boys become conscious of the fact that it was there. This was because a sketch pad was as much a part of Lee as his clothes. They were so accustomed to seeing the pad under his arm that they would have been more likely to notice its absence than its presence there.

Now, however, they realized that this was the same pad he had dug out of the pile in his studio that morning. Lee opened it to a page of sketches and held it up against the wall alongside the Arnold photo. The instant he did so, his eyes lit up.

"Sure. The eyes, the nose . . . you know, when you're an artist, when you're constantly sketching faces as I am, your eye becomes trained to see the basic structure of a face to more of an extent than most people do."

His voice throbbed with conviction as he went on.

"Do you know what I think? I think Skinny Arnold has spent twenty years growing about as nearly perfect a disguise as anybody could think of!"

"No," said Lee, "I don't mean he did it on purpose —"

"Of course not," said Harvey, leaning across the booth in the drugstore where they were having doughnuts and coffee. "Why, the whole thing fits together now like a dream. He escapes to South America and stays there, picking up a living somehow — probably not too honestly. He keeps thinking of getting his hands on the loot buried on the island, but knows he doesn't dare slip back into the country and turn up around here. Years go by. He begins to get fat. One day he realizes that maybe Nature is solving his problem for him. He's smart enough to be patient, so he waits, and keeps getting fatter."

"Finally the thirty-year-old skinny man has become a fifty-year-old fat man," said Lee. "The perfect disguise!"

"Or anyway, it should have been, if it weren't for a crazy artist," grinned Skip.

Lee doodled thoughtfully on a corner of his sketch pad.

"Don't forget, though," he cautioned, "our whole theory could still be as cockeyed as one of Harvey's plays."

"Hey! I resent that," declared the playwright.

"Quiet, Shakespeare. The fact remains that I couldn't swear on a stack of Bibles that Doc Dillingham is Skinny Arnold. The resemblance I see could be merely a coincidence. We have a brilliant theory, but no facts. We could get ourselves into a peck of trouble if we went around now suggesting that Doc Dillingham, our popular visiting ornithologist, is a thief and a killer."

"Mr. Eph would personally flay us alive," agreed Harvey. "All right, so what we need now is some facts. The question is, then, how do we go about gathering them?"

"Well, for a starter, I'd like to have a look at those diggings out on Tree House Island myself," said Lee.

"That's tricky."

"I know . . . I wonder if you fellows could get away for an all-night outing if you told your folks that you were going with me?"

The boys exchanged a glance.

"I don't see why not."

128

"Neither do I."

"An all-night outing on the beach out near the Point was what I had in mind," added Lee.

The boys stared at him with their hearts beating faster as the implications of his suggestion became clear.

"Swell," said Skip. "But even at night, someone would hear our motor if we tried to go out, specially with the on-shore breeze we'll probably have."

"That's right. So what we need is a canoe," said Lee. Both boys nodded.

"Good idea," said Skip. "Moon doesn't rise till ten-thirty tonight, and it should be dark enough to start out by ten."

"The next question is, where can we get the canoe?" asked Harv.

Lee's face twitched. He took his pipe out of his mouth, peered into its bowl, and remarked, "Gumbo's would be perfect."

"Oh, boy!" Harvey's tone was dubious. "You'll never get Gumbo's canoe without Gumbo."

"So much the better. Let him come along."

The boys were flabbergasted.

"Lee! Are you crazy?"

"Certainly not." Lee's eyes twinkled with a completely sane light. "Look, if Mr. Eph heard the three of us had gone out to the Point on an all-night camping trip, he might smell a rat. It might occur to him that we were suspiciously close to Tree House Island. But not even Mr. Eph would ever think we could be up to anything very serious if we took Gumbo along!"

129

10

Before they left Lanfield, Lee drove up Main Street a couple of blocks and pointed out the Lanfield First National Bank.

"That's where it happened. Their car pulled up here on the corner, and they ran inside through those doors."

Skip was no Harvey, but as he looked at the actual scene of the crime he had no trouble imagining the car's sudden stop, the rush inside, and then the sharp crack of the shots, just before the men rushed out again and the car raced away. He thought of the old guard lying on the floor, his gun useless beside his stiffening hand . . .

"I guess there's a lot of us who'd like to see them finally catch the guy that killed poor old Gus," declared Lee. Harvey nodded. They had all been sharing the same thoughts.

"Well, Doc Dillingham may not be the man, but we'll make darn sure he's not, before we're through," said Lee as he drove on. His mouth curled sardonically around the stem of his pipe. "We've certainly worked ourselves into a sweet fix. If we're wrong about Doc and we slip up in any way, our goose will be cooked to a fare-thee-well. Harvey here will blow his chance for a scholarship and probably be exiled to Boston for good measure."

"That's for sure."

"And when your father gets through with you, Skip, you'll be on the beach with no boat of your own. And as for me, Mr. Eph will tag me as an irresponsible troublemaker and run me out of my studio, and everybody else will be forced to agree that he's right."

"That's a cheerful prospect, all around," remarked Harvey.

"On the other hand," said Lee slowly, "if we're *right* about Doc . . ."

"Well?"

"If we're right about him, then we're fooling with a criminal who has killed at least once and probably wouldn't hesitate to kill again if anybody got in his way while he was reaching for a hundred thousand bucks. Or maybe he'd have Professor Santos do the dirty work for him. At any rate, if we are right and Doc gets wind of the fact that we're suspicious and nosing around, we're going to be in a very precarious situation."

"However," said Harvey, "I don't see that just going out there and looking at their diggings again is likely to give us the kind of evidence we really need. I think we've got to go further than that."

"What do you mean?"

Harvey's eyes were gleaming with the light of high adventure behind the thick black-rimmed glasses, but there was no quality of play-acting about him now. He was well aware of the risks involved as he made his startling proposal.

"I think we've got to get over on that island and hide out there till they come again."

For a moment there was silence in the car. Then Skip whistled softly.

"Boy!"

"Now, *there's* a way to spend a relaxing evening," said Lee.

"Well, what about it, though?" insisted Harvey. "How else can we really hope to learn the facts? Look, we can go out there in the canoe the minute it's dark —"

"What if they're already there before dark?"

"I'm hoping they'll follow the same routine as last night. Remember, they didn't come over last night until after dark. Until after the moon was up, in fact."

"That's true. Well, anyway, go ahead."

"Okay. We go out the minute it's dark. We hide the canoe alongside the black boulder, under the bushes that hang over the water there. We hide ourselves, and wait. If they show up, we watch, and listen. After they finish digging and leave, we wait until we can't hear their boat any more. Then we take off, and nobody's the wiser — except maybe us."

Lee nodded.

"It's risky, but it's our best bet."

"I'm for it," agreed Skip.

"All right, then. Now, next let's plan our outing and decide what we need to take along to make it look good — besides Gumbo, that is!"

132

Back in Goose Harbor, they dropped Harvey off first.

"Get busy and work your tail off, Harv, so you can sure go tonight," advised Skip.

"I will. I'll work so hard I'll give Aunt Sarah something new to worry about. She'll think I'm sick."

Harvey loped away around the side of the inn to the kitchen door, moving with his usual disjointed appearance, as though he might fly apart at any minute. Skip chuckled.

"What a guy!"

"He's not lacking in gumption, either," was Lee's opinion as they drove on. "I think he'd be all right in a pinch."

"I'd be willing to gamble on it. Gee, I hope we're right about this business, though, if only because of the way it would make a lot of people around here change their tune about him."

"I expect it would, at that."

They passed the Goose Harbor Cooperative Bank, and glanced silently at its quietly prosperous façade.

"I wish that old geezer in there would change his tune about *me*," remarked Lee.

"Well," said Skip, "stranger things have happened — though I don't know what."

Lee laughed, and gunned the old beach wagon up the hill to the parsonage.

"Be sure to get Gumbo lined up right away for the big outing of the Goose Harbor Marching and Chowder Society," said Lee, when Skip had jumped out.

"You really think we need him?"

133

"Why not? He's all right, and he'll give the whole thing an innocent look."

Skip sighed.

"Well, I'd probably never be able to talk him out of his canoe, anyway, once he found out what was up — and he'd find out."

Skip hurried into the house to make sure that he could go on an overnight outing that night himself, but found that neither his father nor mother was home. He fixed himself a peanut butter sandwich, gulped a glass of milk, and headed for Gumbo's, finishing the sandwich as he went.

He found the boy mechanic lying on his back under his latest custom-built car, which was propped up on two boxes so he could get his head under it. A pistol-like bubble-gum pop indicated he had clearance enough to indulge his pet habit.

"Hi, Skip," he said, when he had twisted enough to get a glimpse of his visitor. "I'm putting in those power brakes."

"Power brakes, yet?"

"Yeah. I furnish the power."

Skip peered under at him.

"What's the idea of this arrangement? Why don't you just turn her over on her side to work on her?"

Gumbo gave him a disgusted look.

"Listen, when I start working on real cars I'll have to crawl under them, won't I? There's no time like the present to start practicing!"

Skip sat down on an old fish barrel Gumbo had lugged home from a recent beachcombing expedition.

"Listen, Gumbo. Lee Rand and Harv and I are going out to the Point to camp overnight."

The car trembled from the impact of a hard head as Gumbo forgot himself and tried to sit up.

"Ow!" He wriggled out from under and stood up holding his forehead. "Tonight? Can I go along?"

"If you want to."

"Sure!"

"We want to take along your canoe, too."

"Yeah? Why?"

"Well . . . we may have use for it. Never mind about that now. We'll explain everything after we get out there."

"But —"

"Yes or no, Gumbo?"

"Okay!" said Gumbo — and immediately went on to guess

the purpose of the expedition. "Going over to the island, huh?"

"Ssh! Not so loud!" cried Skip sternly, glancing around the small back yard. "Listen, you keep your mouth shut from now till we leave, see? We don't want anyone to get any funny ideas."

"Okay, okay, I will."

"Is your canoe on the beach?"

"Yes."

"Okay. Be at Lee's at six o'clock."

"You bet!"

Having made sure of Gumbo — and his canoe — Skip returned home and climbed to the loft in the small garage and barn behind the parsonage. His tent was stored there. They had decided it was a good idea to take along the tent and all the other trappings of an outing, to make it look good, whether they ever used them all or not. They would pitch a tent, build a fire, cook chow — go through all the motions of an ordinary camping trip. He lowered the rolled-up tent to the barn floor and laid it in readiness across a pair of sawhorses.

Next it seemed a good idea to ride down to the harbor and make sure the *Fifteen* was all ready for the short but important trip over to the Point. He swung aboard his bike, headed down the hill, and turned into Front Street. He nodded and spoke to several persons along the way.

He tried to look as unconcerned as possible, but felt just the opposite as he thought about how all those people would buzz if they knew what he and his friends were planning to do that night. The responsibility of it suddenly weighed heavily on him. There were always plenty of people around who were looking for an excuse to criticize the minister and his family. Mr. Wixon, now, just hurrying out of the bank on some errand or other — how he would wag his head and nod knowingly if he heard that Skip Ellis and Harvey Harding were in trouble again!

Skip looked ahead along the familiar street and was struck by the thought that after tonight he might never again be able to ride along it and be taken for granted the way he was now. If anything went wrong . . .

"Nuts!" he muttered, and swung around the corner toward the wharf. He would cross all those bridges when he came to them.

Lee was on the beach with his boat. He had pulled her ashore and was turning her over to empty the water out of her.

"Hasn't that scow of yours tightened up yet?" snorted Skip.

"I'll thank you to tighten up that lip of yours," retorted Lee. "She's fine now. Just needed to have a little water stand in her overnight. Did you find Gumbo?"

"Yep. He's all set. Wild horses couldn't keep him away."

"Good. I see his canoe's right here."

"Yes, he said it was."

The *Fifteen* was in good order at all points, so Skip decided to go home again and hang around to see if there was anything anybody was expecting him to do there. He didn't want to get hung up on any last-minute chores.

"I'll drive up about six and bring down your gear," said

137

Lee. "Between you and Gumbo you'll have quite a bit."

"If I know Gumbo, we'll have plenty," said Skip. "See you later."

He had turned to go when a blast on an automobile horn invited them to take notice of a small, pretty girl with snapping eyes in a battered convertible that had appeared on the road at the head of the beach. She waved.

"Hi, Skip."

"Hi, Mary." Skip waved and glanced at Lee, who had apparently found something very interesting to look at inside his boat, and was doing so with a grim expression. Never one to let anybody keep her away from what she wanted to do, Mary jumped out of her car and came down onto the beach. Lee lifted his head to growl an opinion at Skip.

"This beach ought to be restricted."

"Well, if it isn't Daredevil Rand!" said Mary, with a toss of her head. Her cheeks were pink with embarrassment, but as usual she stood her ground. "What are you two up to now?"

"We're going on an overnight camping trip — Harv and Gumbo are going, too," explained Skip.

"Oh? Well, you boys will be in good hands. Mr. Rand is not one to take chances, believe you me."

Skip glanced at Lee, and marveled at his self-control as his jaw remained clamped shut. What would her face have looked like if he suddenly told her how wrong she was, and why?

Mary turned to Skip.

"I thought maybe you'd give me that ride in the *Fifteen*, but I guess this isn't the time."

138

"I've got to get home and make sure the coast is clear for tonight," admitted Skip. "How about tomorrow afternoon for sure, if . . ." he hesitated, and then added quickly, "if you can make it?"

"It's a date. Come on, I'll give you a lift home."

"Thanks."

"Good-by, Daredevil." Mary laughed lightly and walked away toward the car. Skip shot a sympathetic glance back at Lee and tagged along beside her.

When they had driven out of sight, however, her bravado melted away, and her eyes were troubled.

"I guess he's pretty mad at me."

Skip squirmed. "Well, I don't know . . ."

"The heck you don't. Darn him, anyway! If only he weren't so — so conservative. If only he were willing to stick his neck out once in a while!"

Now it was Skip who had to clamp his jaw shut. It was all he could do not to burst out and tell her exactly how far Lee was about to stick his neck out that very night. It was a lucky thing that they had reached his house by then. Mary pulled up, and he jumped out.

"Well, anyway, have fun on your outing, Skip."

She looked like a very little girl with big sad eyes. Skip took pity on her.

"Listen, Mary, you've got the wrong idea about Lee. Wait a little, and give him a chance," he said earnestly. "Just give him a chance."

He waved and jumped the fence into his yard, leaving her

big eyes to grow even rounder and not quite so sad as his earnest reassurance gave her heart a lift.

Skip's father was home now and at work in his study. The study door was open, signifying that he was not trying to sweat out next Sunday's sermon or anything of that sort, so Skip stopped in the doorway.

"Hi, Dad."

His father glanced up from the letter he was writing and smiled.

"Well, Skip. Where have you been all day?"

"Oh, Lee Rand had to drive over to Lanfield, so Harv and I rode with him."

"Lee, eh?" Mr. Ellis regarded Skip thoughtfully. "Do you by any chance know anything about the difficulties he and Mary seem to be having?"

"Well, yes. I know Mr. Eph doesn't approve of him and wants to break things up between them. How did you hear about it, Dad? Did Mary talk to you?"

"Yes."

"She's pretty mad."

The minister laughed sadly. "Yes. In some ways she's not unlike her grandfather."

"That's what Lee says." Skip sat down on the edge of a chair. "Do you think you can pour some oil on troubled waters and help them, Dad?"

"I'll do what I can, but I don't know. I'm not looking forward to talking to her grandfather about it. He's not going to like what I have to say — because I think Lee's a first-rate young man, and nothing irresponsible about him."

140

Certain uneasy thoughts went through Skip's head concerning how his father's mind might be changed if they got into trouble that night, but he tried not to let his uneasiness show in his expression.

"I'm glad you feel that way, Dad." He cleared his throat. "By the way, we're cooking up an overnight camping trip, if that's all right. Lee's going with us."

Mr. Ellis glanced at him with what might have been a glimmer of suspicion. Skip waited, holding his breath, fearful that his father would start asking some embarrassing questions.

"We?" said the minister. "Who's we?"

"Harv and Gumbo and I."

If Mr. Ellis had been suspicious, he obviously relaxed now.

"Gumbo, eh?" He chuckled. "Good idea — a few laughs ought to make Lee feel better. Well, if it's all right with your mother it's all right with me," he added, while Skip silently paid tribute to Lee's sound psychology in including Gumbo.

Shortly before six Lee drove up to the parsonage and they loaded the tent into the back end of the station wagon. Skip tossed his pack in beside it, and rode the tailgate around the corner to Gumbo's. A whistle brought the small boy staggering around the side of his house carrying an enormous pack.

"For Pete's sake, Gumbo, we're not going to Nova Scotia for a month, we're just going to the Point overnight."

"Even so, I have to take some food and a few things. Just a minute, I'll be right back."

141

Gumbo scampered off and returned with a mountainous blanket roll.

"Commodore Gumbo Phillips off to the North Pole," commented Lee.

Gumbo slung the blanket roll aboard and snapped his fingers.

"Oh, I almost forgot. Back in half a sec," he declared, and again he sped away. He whizzed back at high speed with a bulky canvas carrying-bag over his shoulder. "Few important things I couldn't get into my pack," he explained.

He scrambled up onto the tailgate beside Skip, and they rolled down the hill toward the harbor. Lee drove out onto the wharf and they unloaded their gear. There was no sign of Harvey anywhere. Skip glanced around worriedly.

"Gee, I hope nothing's happened to hold up Harv."

"Did you check with him?"

"Yes, I phoned him about an hour ago and he said it looked as if he could make it. But you know how things are at the inn. Something might always come up to keep him home."

"Well, let's hope not," said Lee. "Gumbo, get your canoe and bring her over to the float. We'll stow your stuff aboard and you can get a head start."

"Why can't we just bring his stuff out in the *Fifteen* and let him travel light, Lee?" asked Skip.

"I want to take my own stuff," said Gumbo.

Lee grinned at Skip. "You should have known that. Gumbo, let's compromise — you take your blanket roll and that canvas bag, and Skip'll bring your pack."

142

Gumbo gave in to this arrangement, and was soon along-side the float and loaded, ready to go.

"Gee, where's Harv?" he wondered. "I hope he doesn't forget to bring his telescope."

"He won't. Harv doesn't forget things. Now get going."

"I specially want to watch Mars rise tonight," he declared. "I looked up the time in the almanac, and —"

"Shove off!" ordered Skip, giving the bow of the canoe a shove out into open water.

"Okay, okay," said Gumbo, and paddled away.

They carried the rest of their gear down to the float, and brought Lee's boat and the *Fifteen* over to load them up. Lee tested his five-horse outboard motor and found it in good order. When everything was aboard, they climbed back up on the wharf to look for Harvey.

"I sure hope nothing's gone wrong," said Skip. "Maybe I'd better run down to the inn and check."

"Go ahead."

Skip rounded the corner into Front Street and skidded to a stop at the sight of Harvey Harding, with his pack and blanket roll on his back, standing and talking to Mr. Eph.

It was a sight that gave him some unpleasant qualms until Mr. Eph startled him by doing an almost unheard-of thing. He laughed.

"Gumbo Phillips, hey?" he said. "Well, you certainly ought to have your hands full!"

Chuckling, the old gentleman walked on. Harvey hurried forward, and grinned as he saw Skip.

"Oh — hi, Skip."

"Hi. We were beginning to worry about you."

"Sorry I'm late," said Harvey, as they turned the corner, "but first I almost got stuck at the inn, and then Mr. Eph stopped me to find out where I was going. Say, you know, Lee was right about taking Gumbo —"

"You're telling me!"

By the time they had joined Lee, stowed Harvey's gear in the *Fifteen*, and were ready to go, Gumbo was a small dot out near the harbor entrance. The tide was low, and the water was placid under the slanting rays of the late afternoon sun. The first suggestion of an evening onshore breeze was beginning to stir the air.

They stepped into their boats and glanced at one another.

"I wonder how we'll feel when we come back from this trip?" said Lee. The question had been in all their minds. He grinned, and shook his head. "Maybe it's better not to know. Come on — let's shove off."

11

Immediately to the south of the Point, the beach smoothed out. Above the beach, on hard ground, Lee and the boys made camp. For a while they were busy pitching the tent, collecting driftwood for a fire, and getting the fire started so the cook could go to work.

Harvey was their camp cook. He always learned a good deal about anything that came his way, so naturally he had picked up considerable knowledge of cooking in the kitchen of the inn. He set up a small portable grill and soon had hamburgers grilling, baked beans heating, and home-fried potatoes sizzling in a skillet. Skip and Lee gathered mussels from the rocks at the Point and set a panful on the grill to steam.

They had miles of beach to themselves. To the north, across the mouth of the harbor, a point of light was visible near the shore. That, they knew, was Toby Henderson's place, he being a retired lawyer who was generally the first of the summer folk to show up. To the south, the beach was completely dark; the Wamset Beach colony of cottages would not begin to fill up until the following week. On the highlands

145

behind them, the boys could see a few lights twinkling in the distance. Otherwise they were alone in the world.

As they busied themselves, the shadow of the Point crept out farther and farther across the water, pointing silently at Tree House Island. Checking the island through his telescope, Harvey could see no sign of either the men or their boat.

"I wish we could go out there right now and be sure of getting there first," said Skip. "I keep expecting to see the *Leeway* show up any minute."

"Even if we dared sneak out now," said Lee, "it wouldn't do any good. It would be too risky, trying to hide the canoe and ourselves out there before dark."

"We're going out to the island, huh, Lee?" said Gumbo. "I knew that was it!"

"I just want to have a look at what's doing out there myself. And while we're on the subject," added Lee, "this is the way I think we ought to operate. I think Harv and I should go out to the island while you and Gumbo stand by here with the boats, Skip."

"Aw, shucks!" said Gumbo. "I want to go out there, too!"

"No, four of us is too many," said Skip. He was disappointed, but sensible enough to see that Lee's suggestion made the best arrangement. "Let's do it Lee's way."

"If we signal with our flashlights, that means we need help quick," said Lee. "If we give you three longs, come out as fast as you can in the *Fifteen*, Skip. If you see three shorts, go call out the Coast Guard and the police. Gumbo, if you see

146

three shorts after Skip has come out, *you* go get the Coast Guard. Okay?"

"What about if you should want me to come out, too?"

"Well — if we want you, too, we'll signal long short long."

Gumbo was downcast over being elected rear guard, but he accepted his orders.

"Well, okay, Lee. You're the boss," he declared with a heavy sigh. And they went over the signals again, to make sure they all had them straight.

Before long they were ready to eat. They fell to with a good appetite, but without quite giving their food the whole-hearted attention it would normally have received. Throughout the meal their glances kept turning in the direction of the island, and their ears strained constantly to catch the sound of a motor. The onshore breeze was steadily freshening. It rustled the low trees around them, and stirred the water.

"With this wind we should hear them coming the minute they leave Doane Island," remarked Skip.

"No surprises this time," agreed Harvey.

The first stars appeared, and were promptly studied by Gumbo through the telescope. Harvey carefully put out their fire, so that it would not call attention to their presence on the Point after dark. The sky deepened to a royal blue and then faded to charcoal gray. Tree House Island drew the night about it like a cloak and disappeared.

Lee stood up. He looked at the luminous dial of his watch. "Ten o'clock. Let's go."

For once even Gumbo was too excited to talk. Silently the

four rose and went down the beach to the boats. The tide was beginning to come in now. Pushed by the breeze, small waves rolled in around their bare feet as they ran the canoe out into the water. Lee and Harvey swung themselves in and picked up paddles.

"Good luck," said Skip in a low voice. "Take care."

"So long," whispered Gumbo.

They stood at the water's edge, with wavelets breaking against their shins, and watched the canoe disappear into the dark. With the moon not yet risen, the night was conveniently black.

"Now," said Skip. "If only Doc and the professor don't turn up out of nowhere before they can get out there."

With Lee and Harvey paddling carefully, the canoe slid through the water with scarcely a sound. They were listening harder than ever, dreading the mutter of the *Leeway*'s motor. But except for the occasional squawk of a heron as it rushed by overhead in the darkness they heard nothing.

As Harvey shifted his feet in the bow he felt his heel squash into something. Between strokes his hand made a quick investigation. He grinned to himself. That Gumbo! He had brought so much stuff he couldn't keep track of it all. He had forgotten to take his canvas carrying-bag out of the canoe.

There was not much time to muse about Gumbo's crazy ways, however. The sea was restless now, and they had to pay attention to their handling of the canoe. Even so, they made good time, and were presently sliding alongside the great black boulder that jutted out over the water a few yards from the tiny beach. Slipping into the water up to their waists, they worked the canoe in under the overhanging bushes until it was completely out of sight, and secured it. Then they took their flashlights out of the canoe, clipped them onto the belts of their shorts, and waded ashore. By then their eyes had become accustomed to the darkness to an extent that made the beach seem almost bright.

They had agreed beforehand that they would take a look around first and then settle themselves in their hiding-places, so there was no need to talk as they went ashore. Lee was to choose a spot in the brush a few yards off the trail. As for Harvey, his suggestion for his hiding-place had first been laughed at and then, after he had given his arguments, been accepted.

"The tree house has several advantages," Harvey had declared, when they were discussing hiding-places. "For one thing, it's smack in the center of the island — and that's where they've been doing most of their digging. For another, what would ever make them think anybody might be up there in the middle of the night?"

"Nothing, I suppose — unless you fall out," said Skip. "Still, I don't know. You're really stuck, up there."

"You're stuck anyway, if anything goes wrong, on such a small island," Harvey pointed out.

Harvey led the way up the path now, and peered around him with sharp interest when they reached the lone big tree. Even in the darkness he could see that an amazing amount of additional probing and digging had taken place since the men had caught Skip and him on the island, two nights

149

before. He mentioned the fact to Lee in a low murmur.

"How about having a look with your flashlight?" he added.

Lee's flashlight had a red filter snapped over the end of it. By its dull red glow, as they held it close to the ground, they could discover further details about the digging.

"Look, Lee. They've been going at it scientifically. See how they've marked off squares of ground to be investigated?"

"Yes, and I notice something else, too."

"So do I," nodded Harvey.

Lee played the light around the four sides of a square of undisturbed ground. It was close to the big tree on the offshore side — and it looked like the last marked-off square yet to be investigated.

While they stood looking down at it, a slight, far-off murmur reached their ears. Lee snapped off the light, and they listened.

"It's them."

"Right. Let's take cover."

Harvey sprang up the tree and disappeared into the tree house. Lee walked off the trail in a wide circle, being careful to disturb the underbrush as little as possible, and settled himself to wait and listen.

The smooth burble of the motor steadily grew in volume. Harvey peeped out of the tree house to watch the *Leeway* approach. Behind her a huge gibbous moon was rising, a great lopsided orange ball not yet quite clear of the sea. Cutting through water suddenly aglow with moonlight, the boat came steadily on. Slowly, unhurriedly, she rounded the side of the

150

small island and the professor drove her nose gently up onto the sloping sand of the postage-stamp beach. Both men stepped out of the boat carrying dark lanterns and shovels. The lanterns were a peculiar kind that shed a dim, masked glow in a circle on the ground.

Doc's vague bulk, and a slinking shadow that was the professor, moved up the beach and along the trail. Doc walked slowly, and with huge rumbling sighs, as though every step made him ache. Professor Santos stayed on his heels with obvious impatience.

"Santos, don't rush me," snapped Doc over his shoulder. "I warn you, don't rush me. I've already pushed myself just about as far as I can push."

Again, it was "Santos." Harvey, listening in the tree house, was more certain than ever that the small dark man was no professor.

"All this dig, dig, dig," growled Santos disgustedly. "We dig the whole middle, not find."

"No, Santos, not the whole middle," Doc reminded him as they reached the clearing under the tree. He shone his light on the unmarked square of earth. "This has to be it."

"And what if it's not?"

Doc's breath went snorting out of him heavily. "Well, if not, then we'll start digging around the outside edge of what we've already checked. It's here somewhere, and we're going to find it. That cursed hurricane! If only I'd had those three trees to go by, I could have lined up the exact spot right away — but with only one tree left, and no way to be sure it's even one of the three I took my bearings on . . . !"

151

He called the island several unscientific names, and told Santos to start probing. Together they twisted the long, thin bore into the ground, laboriously, time after time. There was something frightening and dreadful about their terrible determination.

For a long time the only sounds were Doc's groans, and the deep rumble of his voice as he cursed under his breath. In the tree house a large ant chose that time to drop on Harvey's neck and crawl down under his tee shirt. Harv gritted his teeth and steeled himself to endure whatever tickling or chewing he was in for as the six small legs moved along his backbone.

The ant had reached the base of his spine and was bringing sweat to Harv's brow as he struggled not to move a muscle in spite of the prickly torture, when Doc uttered an excited exclamation.

"There! That's metal. I'll swear that's metal. Here, dig here!"

Santos needed no urging. He had already seized a shovel. As Doc stood aside with the bore, Santos went to work. Doc picked up a dark lantern and held it waist high while he watched. It leaked enough light to add a feeble glow to the pale moonlight and starlight by which they were working.

Santos's spade bit greedily into the earth. The hole it was making widened and deepened. And with each spadeful Doc seemed to bend forward more eagerly over the hole.

The spade clanked on metal.

The dull, hard impact was unmistakable. Its effect on Doc made Harvey feel almost as though he were watching the ceremonies of some dark religion. The way the fat man

152

dropped to his knees beside the hole was like a hideous parody
of prayer. A few more shovelfuls, and Doc brushed Santos's
spade aside.

"Look out!" he ordered, and seemed about to enter the
hole headfirst in his eagerness to reach down and feel the
object the spade had struck. He scrabbled in the earth with
his hands, digging like a dog, uncovering their find. Muffled,
but triumphant, his words came — "Yes! Yes!"

Santos had dropped to his knees beside him now. Together
they worked, heads down in the hole, grunting and tugging,
until Doc said, "I've got a handle. Find the handle on the
other end. . . . That's it!"

With one final effort they heaved a box up out of the hole
and set it on the ground. It was a rectangular, black, rust-
encrusted box about two feet long.

"Tools. Get the tools," ordered Doc, and Santos flashed down the trail to the beach. Strange low chuckles of deep excitement rumbled up out of the fat man's vast interior, like waves telling of a distant storm, and his hands ran over the box as though he were caressing a living thing. When Santos returned, Doc seized the tools from him and went to work. A few moments later the lid creaked and grated as, by means of sheer strength not to be denied, the two men forced it open.

Up to that moment, in spite of ants, muscle ache, and excitement, Harvey had managed not to move. Now he moved. He was in such a fever of curiosity to see what was in the box that he shifted his position slightly.

The floor of the tree house creaked.

Harv froze. Below him, neither man glanced up or noticed the sound. Because both had uttered a gasp at the same instant.

The risk Harv had taken was wasted effort. He still could not see into the box. The fat man's great round body blocked his view completely.

"Lovely, lovely," Doc was muttering. "I'd forgotten how beautiful it could be . . ."

"*Santa Maria!*" murmured Santos. "*Madre de Dios!*"

Then Doc brought his excitement under control. His voice was brisk and nearly normal again as he began to close the lid.

"Let's go, Professor," he said, with a hearty chuckle. "I think our research is finished."

Santos uttered an unexpected, high-pitched, elated cackle.

154

Together they forced the lid down again. When they stood up and Harvey could see the box, it was completely closed.

"Now, let's fill up our final hole, Santos."

"The devil with the hole!"

Doc's voice was suddenly sharp and hard again.

"The devil with nothing! We'll fill up the hole, and take away every tool, and overlook no detail. The less we leave for anyone to wonder about, the better."

Santos shrugged and took up the shovel. He was in too good a mood at that point to argue.

When he had filled in the hole to Doc's satisfaction, the fat man said, "Now, pick up all the tools and the lanterns and let's go. I can handle the box."

Before he stooped to pick up the box, Doc held up his wrist and peered at his watch.

"Ten to twelve," he remarked, and chuckled with immense satisfaction. "A brief evening's work for a change, Professor — a brief evening's work!"

Keeping watch on the beach had been as unexciting as it was frustrating. For a long time Skip and Gumbo stared tensely out into the darkness, wondering if they would suddenly see three long flashes, or three short ones. They listened, but the tumble and hiss of waves breaking on the beach as the tide came in made it hard to be sure of any faint sounds the onshore breeze might be carrying to them over fifteen hundred yards of ruffled water. At one point they thought they heard the murmur of a far-off motorboat, just as

155

the moon was rising, but it could have been their imagination.

Though Gumbo tried the telescope periodically, it was of little help in penetrating the darkness between them and the island. A low cloud bank had drifted across the horizon, and scattered clouds scudding along higher up prevented the moon from being of much help. Gumbo lay on his back with his knees raised and the telescope balanced on them while he trained it on the spot where, from time to time, Polaris, the North Star, appeared.

"Tell me any time you want to be relieved, and I'll take over the watch, Skip."

"Okay."

"Hey, what time is it?"

"Almost midnight. Why?"

"I just remembered something. I want to watch Mars rise tonight. Sometimes he's real red then."

"What time's he due to rise?"

"Twelve-o-six. I've got my alarm clock set for twelve sharp to remind me so's I wouldn't forget."

Skip snorted. "You mean to say you brought along an alarm clock, too?"

"Sure! Why not?"

"Listen, for Pete's sake let's not have any alarm clocks going off around here tonight! What's the matter with you, anyway?"

"Don't get excited. With this onshore breeze, who's going to hear it but us?"

"Never mind that. Just go get it and shut it off."

"Okay, okay! You don't have to get sore."

"Where is it?"

"Oh, it's around here somewhere," said Gumbo. "It's in my canvas bag."

12

Santos gathered up the tools. Doc picked up the box, and followed the small man down the path. They put everything aboard, shoved the boat off, and scrambled in. Santos started the motor, and began to back the boat off into deep water. Another moment now, and they would be gone.

Up in his tree house perch, Harvey was thinking of a dozen things at once, planning what to suggest to Lee as their best move. Should they signal for Skip to pick them up, and then go try to convince the police or the Coast Guard that . . . that what? That a man they thought was a bank robber and killer was out on Doane Island with a box that might contain a hundred thousand dollars of stolen money? By the time they did that, Doc and Santos might easily have picked up their stuff on Doane Island and vanished.

On the other hand, perhaps the men would play it cool now and not leave until tomorrow. Maybe they would decide to carry out the game the whole way, and come ashore to leave in broad daylight, with everybody still accepting them as visiting ornithologists. In that case it would be better to slip ashore in the canoe and not take a chance on their hearing the *Fifteen* come out.

The *Leeway*'s propeller churned in the water, reversing her momentum. She began to move forward. Harvey checked the time. Four minutes to twelve.

The *Leeway* picked up speed and disappeared around the side of the island. As the sound of her motor dwindled, Harvey watched the boat from his high perch, able to see her wake in the moonlight each time the moon found an opening in the clouds.

He had his foot on the first crosspiece, ready to start down, when he heard a low laugh.

"Harv?" Lee had appeared on the trail beneath him. "Man, was I glad to see that pair get going! Come on, we'd better —"

"Wait a minute!" Harvey was watching the *Leeway*, watching her wake bend in a tight curve that put his heart back in his mouth again. "I'm afraid I've got bad news, Lee. I think they're coming back!"

"What! You mean it?"

"Yes! They're coming! Take cover again," said Harvey, scrambling back into the tree house.

A tense moment passed, during which the sound of the motor grew steadily louder. The *Leeway* rounded into the miniature cove, and as Santos cut the motor they could hear Doc's voice, grating with irritation.

"I told you to pick up everything, and by that I meant everything. Now find that bore and make it snappy. I don't operate sloppy, and I never will."

159

The instant the boat touched the sand Santos was out and running up onto the island. Cursing, he searched for the bore, found it, and returned. Erect on the center thwart, Doc slumped into a more relaxed mountain of a man and flashed his genial smile.

"Good. Now, then —"

BR-R-R-R-R-R-RING!

No sound could have been more shattering. One instant Doc was slumped in his seat, smiling contentedly, and Santos was bending forward to shove the boat off. The next instant Santos had dropped flat on the sand, and Doc was on his feet with a gun in his hand.

Br-r-r-r-r-ring!

The sound continued, the out-of-place, early-morning sound of an alarm clock. Doc crouched in the boat, waiting, and Santos lifted himself slowly on his hands, turning his dark face toward the jangling bell, as slowly the alarm ran down and stopped.

For a moment it left stunned silence. Then Doc barked into the darkness.

"Who's there? Show yourself, or I'll shoot!"

Silence. Doc glanced at Santos, and jerked his head in the direction the sound had come from. Santos slid forward like something half reptilian, and the pale, cold flicker of bright steel betrayed the knife he held ready.

His investigation was cautious, thorough, and one step at a time. Inevitably, he made a discovery.

"Boat!" he called.

Doc stepped out of the *Leeway*, pulled the bow up onto

160

shore so she would not drift off, and went to join Santos.

"A canoe, eh?"

Santos was giving the canoe a quick once-over. He pulled the canvas bag from under the thwart and held it up. Doc took it and looked inside. He brought out an alarm clock.

"Here we are." He rummaged around in the bag some more and pulled out several small packages. "Gum. Bubble gum. Who was that kid . . . ? Gumbo, they called him. Some of those kids must be here."

Doc began to chuckle heartily. He walked back toward the *Leeway*, and he was still chuckling as he called out in a loud voice.

"All right, kids! Don't be afraid. We're not mad. We've finished our work here on your island, so we don't mind any more whether you're here or not. You're welcome. So don't be afraid — you can come out of hiding."

Crouched in the tree house, Harvey held his breath. Doc waited for a moment, and though Harvey could not see him clearly, he knew that when next he spoke his smile was no longer there.

"Come on out, kids," he advised in a voice that had gone steely. For Harvey it was uncomfortably easy to imagine how small and vicious his eyes had become. "Don't make us search the island for you, because the Professor's an expert at that. A mouse couldn't get away from him, if he wanted to hunt it down. But we're not in the mood for games just now. So come on out now, kids, and jump into your canoe and go home, and you won't get hurt."

The tree house suddenly seemed extremely small and cage-

161

like to Harvey. He felt absolutely cornered, without a hope of escape. There was nothing he could do but crouch there miserably and wait until Santos found him. And they would find Lee, too, and then . . . what?

"All right!" snapped Doc. "In one minute by my watch I'm going to take a crowbar and go to work on your canoe. Then we'll start looking for you. This is your last chance."

Harvey was wondering if, as a forlorn last hope, he shouldn't cause a sudden loud disturbance that would attract the men to the tree house, and thus give Lee an outside chance to grab the *Leeway* and get going before Doc could shoot him. But before Harvey could move, the underbrush stirred.

Lee walked out onto the trail.

"All right, Dr. Dillingham," he called in a jaunty voice, as though the whole affair were a great joke. "I give up."

A second later he was blinking in a powerful glare as Doc switched on the *Leeway*'s searchlight. Doc trained his gun on the advancing figure.

"Keep coming," he said, "and put your hands up."

Lee laughed. "Look, Doc. I'd hardly be armed, you know."

"The Professor will see about that," said Doc. Santos stepped forward and frisked Lee.

"I don't know where a man wearing shorts would be carrying concealed weapons anyway, for that matter," Lee added.

"All right, put your hands down and tell me what you're doing here. First of all, who are you?"

162

"We met. Don't you remember? On the beach, when you brought your boat."

"Oh, yes. You're the artist."

"That's right. Lee Rand's the name. Really, I'm embarrassed about this, and I won't try to fool you — I'm here out of sheer curiosity."

"Kids been talking to you, I suppose."

"Yes. They couldn't figure out what you were doing out here. Well, of course, I made light of the whole business — but I was curious all the same. I finally decided to sneak out here on my own and have a look. So I borrowed a canoe from one of the kids, and out I came. Then you showed up, and I hid out, hoping to stay clear till you left."

"Is that why you hid the canoe so carefully?" snapped Doc.

Lee grinned. "Well, naturally, if you *did* turn up, I didn't want to be caught flatfooted."

"And what were you doing with an alarm clock, set for — what was it? Midnight?"

"I didn't know it was there. The kid I borrowed the canoe from must have left it in the boat."

"And you came out alone?"

"Why, sure. You don't think I'd have admitted to a bunch of kids that I was curious enough to sneak out here, do you? Why, I'd have felt even sillier than I feel now."

For a moment Doc eyed him narrowly.

"Maybe so," he said finally, "but I don't believe in taking chances, or in taking people's word. I think maybe we'd better check the island, just to make sure."

The fat man glanced around casually, but his small eyes kept darting back to Lee to observe his reactions. Then the tree house, silhouetted dimly against the sky, caught his eye.

"That tree house, now," he said. "One of your young friends could very well be up there."

He turned the searchlight's beam toward the tree. It found the trunk, moved up the ladder, and played over the weathered boards.

"Maybe we should have a look," he decided.

Lee laughed. "Good idea. I'd love to watch you climb up there."

Doc glanced at Santos. "He's full of fun, this one. I like that," he said. Then he faced Lee again — and his hand cut hard across Lee's mouth.

Almost daintily he wiped blood from his knuckles, blood that had come from Lee's lip.

"Leave the jokes about my weight to me," suggested Doc in a silky voice. "I don't care for them coming from others."

The unforeseen, first outward show of violence was as shocking as it was sudden. And Santos, standing silently by, was like an animal that had smelled blood. He moved forward, his eyes glittering.

"No, Santos," said Doc. "Our trespasser will go back to the other island with us. Go have a look in that tree house. I have a feeling our clever friend here was being a bit too clever. I have a feeling I may have hit on something."

Santos turned and padded up the trail to the big tree. He

164

kept his knife in his hand as he went up the ladder. Illuminated by the searchlight, he disappeared into the tree house. Lee looked on, smiling steadily, while Doc kept his distance and watched him.

Five seconds passed. Santos reappeared, dropped quickly down the ladder, and jogged back down the path.

"Well?" said Doc.

Santos shook his head.

Doc glanced at Lee again.

"All right, let's assume you were alone. At any rate, we won't waste any more time here. We'll take the canoe with us, and get going. Get in, Mr. Rembrandt, get in. And don't make me impatient again, because next time I won't use my knuckles."

Skip glanced at his watch.

"You must not have set that clock of yours right, Gumbo. It's midnight now."

Gumbo was rummaging around inside the tent. "Funny, though, I can't find my canvas bag . . ."

All at once he rushed outside clapping his hand to his head.

"My gosh! Maybe I forgot to take it out of my canoe!"

Skip stared up at him.

"Cripes! What if Doc has heard it?"

Gumbo's face was wretched with premonitions of disaster.

"Oh, gosh, Skip! You don't suppose —"

"Look!"

A flash of light had caught Skip's eye. They peered into

the darkness. A light showed vaguely, out toward Tree House Island. It was not turned in their direction, and it was steady.

"What's that?"

"I don't know. Somebody's showing a light — but who?"

"What'll we do?"

"I don't know what to do, yet." Skip stared at the glow with an uneasy feeling in the pit of his stomach. "Let's get the *Fifteen* in the water, though. I'm going to stand offshore, ready to go out if they signal. And you stand by with Lee's boat if I do."

"Gee, if they're in trouble, and I —"

"Never mind that now. Bear a hand here."

They ran the *Fifteen* into the water, and Skip started his motor, lying offshore about ten yards. They watched the glow in silence.

Suddenly it was gone. In blackness they strained eyes and ears.

"I think I hear a motor!" cried Gumbo. "I'm sure I do!"

"I think you're right!" said Skip excitedly. "Golly, it's hard just to sit here."

"Let's go out!"

"No. Not yet. Gumbo, you've got to stay put here, anyway. We've got to have an anchor man."

"Hey, look!" Gumbo pointed wildly. "Three longs!"

They watched. Again, in the darkness, three bright flashes of light.

"Keep watching!" cried Skip, and gunned the *Fifteen*

166

into a turn. He ran the ten up to full speed and laid a course straight for the island.

It was a rough ride over unruly water, but Skip got everything out of the *Fifteen* she had to offer in a fast, wet ride. Out of the darkness ahead appeared a pale blob that was the tiny beach on Tree House Island. The outlines of the island firmed, and grew larger. The flashlight continued to blink from time to time. Soon Skip could make out a familiar figure pacing about impatiently on shore. In another moment the *Fifteen* had reached the beach.

"Skip!" Harv had a badly skinned knee, and his long face looked drawn and pale. His eyes were afire with excitement behind the huge black-rimmed glasses.

"Harv! What happened?"

"They've got Lee!"

"They've what?"

Harvey explained what had happened.

"It's lucky I got away at all. I decided my only chance was to climb up and lie on the roof of the tree house. When Doc hit Lee, that gave me a chance. I swung up onto the roof then, and they were too occupied to notice. I skinned my knee good doing it, but it worked. When Santos climbed up to look in the house I thought I'd have heart failure, though."

"What do you think they'll do to Lee?"

"I don't know — but we've got to get help to him somehow."

"Well, come on, then — hop in and let's go."

"No, wait. Skip, I don't think there's time for that. We've

167

got to help him right away. Even if the police or the Coast Guard reached Doane Island before the men left it, they'd still have Lee as their hostage. If we're right about Doc, he's already a killer, so he'll do anything to keep from getting caught. No, I've been thinking, and I believe there's another way to work it," declared Harvey. Pointing his flashlight toward shore, he began to send long short long, long short long.

"Hey!" cried Skip. "What are you doing? That'll bring Gumbo out here!"

"For this one we'll need everybody," replied Harvey grimly, "even Gumbo."

13

ALONE IN THE *Fifteen*, Harvey drove her slowly across the dark waters toward the patch of light, now only a couple of hundred yards distant, that marked Doane Island. Hunched over the steering handle, he watched the patch grow until it became a square on the ground in front of the cabin.

His long face twisted with a scared grimace as he thought about how surprised the men must be to hear a boat heading their way. His heart pounded harder and harder with each yard of choppy water the big dory covered, and his hand clamped hard on the steering handle grip as though to gain confidence from its steady throb.

When he was within a hundred yards of the beach, a flashlight winked on ashore and swept out across the sea to look for him. A shiver of fear ran down his spine like a monster-size ant as the light found the boat and settled on him, but he drove her steadily on.

Nobody hailed him as he ran the bow of the *Fifteen* onto the beach, but the flashlight bobbed as Doc walked toward him, with Santos at his side. Harvey took a deep breath, thought about all the plays he had ever written and acted in,

169

and stepped out of the boat. Straightening up, holding his bony frame very erect, he marched toward the approaching men, pulling his own flashlight off his belt as he walked. He waited until they were near, and then with a great show of confidence, and with his irrepressible flair for the dramatic, Harvey stopped, planted his feet apart, and spoke.

"Where's Lee Rand?" he demanded in ringing tones, despite a very dry throat. "I know you've got him, and I demand that you let him go!"

Doc's head went back a little at that. But then he wheezed as though with vast amusement.

"Why, lad, what are you talking about?"

Harvey turned and blinked his flashlight in the direction of Tree House Island. A wink of light answered his signal immediately. Doc's tone changed.

"Here, now, what's this?" he demanded angrily.

"Don't try anything funny, that's all," Harvey retorted in a cocksure voice. "Skip and Gumbo are waiting over there with a boat. Now that I've signaled them, you've got exactly five

170

minutes by Skip's watch to hand Lee over. If I'm not on my way back by then, they'll head for shore — and even in the *Leeway* you'll never be able to catch up with them before they get there."

Doc's eyes were mere pouchy slits now in his puffy face. "Now look here, lad —"

Harvey glanced at his watch.

"Four minutes."

Santos growled a few words in Spanish, but Doc shook his head. He stared at Harvey, and began to smile again. He continued to shake his head, and his rich, oily chuckle returned, almost playfully.

"Harvey Harding, you're quite a lad," he declared, "quite a lad. In spite of everything, it's been a privilege to know you. Now, Harvey, I want you to be reasonable and look at this thing for a minute from our side. I suppose you were ashore somewhere close by and knew your friend Lee had sneaked out for a look around —"

"That's right. We camped out for the night on the Point."

"Of course. So you came out and found him gone and decided we had him, is that it? Well, you're right. He was trespassing on our island. At first I was terribly angry. I seriously considered turning him over to the authorities and making a case of it. But now I've decided not to bother. Our work is finished here. Our equipment is all in the *Leeway*, ready to go. We're ready to leave. Now, your friend's all right. He's unharmed. Come on up, and we'll show you. So be reasonable, Harvey. Signal your friends that everything's all right, and we'll release Lee to you, and be on our way. I was pretty mad

171

at him at first, but that was foolish of me. After all, I suppose his curiosity was only natural. How about it, Harvey?"

"Well . . ." Harvey considered. "Do I have your word that you'll let him go, Doc?"

Doc bowed his round head. "You have my word as a gentleman, lad."

"Okay."

Harvey turned and flicked his light. Immediately a blink answered him. He turned to Doc.

"All right. Now where's Lee?"

"Right where you're going to be in about one minute, lad," replied Doc, and his laughter boomed out as Santos darted behind Harvey and pinned his arms against his back with a cruel twist.

"Ow! Hey! You gave me your word!" cried Harvey.

Doc continued to laugh. He patted Harvey on the shoulder.

"You're a fine, clean-cut American boy, lad," he declared mockingly. "Full of all the homespun virtues. For which let us give thanks. Take him up, Santos."

And while Santos jerked Harvey along up to the cabin, Doc strolled behind them enjoying what was, for once, a thoroughly genuine laugh.

Lee was sitting in a chair in the living room of the cabin. He was bound to the chair hand and foot, and Harvey could see at a glance that he had been tied up by an expert. For good measure, his mouth had been taped with wide adhesive. His eyes grew round and horrified as a push from Santos sent Harvey stumbling into the room.

"We have company, Lee," said Doc, still enjoying himself hugely. "Young Harvey Harding dropped in to ask after you. Nice of him, don't you think?"

"Don't you worry," snapped Harvey, glaring at the fat man. "Skip and Gumbo won't wait forever. When I don't come back, they'll get wise quick. And I'll tell you something else, too, Dr. Dillingham," he added hotly. "They know who you are, the same as we do. Being fat won't protect you any more, Mr. . . . Skinny Arnold!"

The fat man's enjoyment ended with a jolt. His broad face went oyster white and blotchy, and for a moment he swayed on his small feet.

His recovery was an amazing exhibition of iron control. Gradually he steadied and grew calm. His shoulders sagged in a tired way, and all last trace of the genial mask he had

173

worn so constantly vanished. He stared at Harvey in a brooding way, and then turned to Santos.

"We'll have to round up those other kids and bring them back here. They're camping out overnight. They won't be expected home until sometime tomorrow. Nobody will get worried and start looking for them before tomorrow night, if then. That will give us plenty of time. Yes, we've got to go grab them, right now. Tie up this one, and let's go."

Santos did a quick, efficient job on Harvey. The ropes bit painfully into his bare arms and legs, and Santos took pleasure in drawing them tight.

Undaunted, Harvey had a final word to say.

"You'll never catch them!" he taunted the fat man. "They'll take off before you even get near them."

Santos tore a strip of adhesive tape and pressed it across Harvey's mouth. For a moment the gross fat man stood looking down at the helpless boy. Then he reached out and carefully removed the thick glasses.

"Never hit a small boy with his glasses on, Santos," he remarked, and slammed his hand across Harvey's face. "That's for being too smart for your own good."

Santos watched, smiling. Doc held up the glasses and deliberately let them slip from his fingers to the floor.

"How clumsy of me," he said, and set his foot on them. Bits of the frames sprang across the room, and the lenses crackled to powder beneath his heel.

"When we get back with the others, I may make a real example of you, Harvey," he remarked with a smile. "Think about that while we're gone."

174

His rolling chuckle was nakedly vicious. Still chuckling, he waddled out of the cabin toward the beach, with Santos at his heels. Behind them, Lee's eyes burned with silent, helpless outrage, and Harvey shook tears of pain onto his cheeks as he cleared his head from the blow and peered nearsightedly at the door.

From outside came the sound of the fat man's voice, lazily scornful.

"No, Santos, you fool. No, you stupid fool, not in the *Leeway*. Don't you know those kids have ears? Don't you know they're used to boats? They can tell the difference between our boat and the *Fifteen* the minute we start the motor. Don't you realize our young friend in there was counting on that? No, I think we'll go over in the *Fifteen*. That should do very nicely — eh, Harvey, my lad?" he called back mockingly. "By the time they realize the wrong people are in her it'll be too late. Oh, yes — and just to be on the safe side, put the chain and padlock on the *Leeway*'s wheel."

Tensed in his chair, Lee slumped dejectedly as he heard all last hopes go a-glimmering. Harvey did his best to say something, but even Harvey could not manage it through tape. He writhed around in his chair. Even if he had still had his glasses he could not have seen what was going on outside. Lee, however, could see the *Fifteen* through the open door. After Santos had tended to the *Leeway*, Lee watched the two men shove the *Fifteen* off and climb into her. The captives listened helplessly to the low mutter of the ten as Santos backed the boat offshore, and then to the smooth forward drive of the motor as he headed her for Tree House Island.

175

Steadily the sound dwindled as the *Fifteen* left Doane Island behind.

A moment passed, the blackest moment of Lee's life. A moment of utter helplessness filled with ugly thoughts of what might take place when the men returned with the other boys . . .

Then a new sound made them prick up their ears. The sound of bare feet padding along outside. Harvey and Lee twisted their necks to look in the direction of the sound, which was approaching the side of the cabin.

Still wet, Skip climbed in through the window carrying his frogman flippers. He took in their strange appearance with an astonished glance, and grinned as he pulled a knife out of the sheath on his swim trunks belt.

"Wish I'd brought my camera," he declared. He bent over Harvey. "Now, this won't hurt much," he said, working a corner of the adhesive tape loose. "The only way to take this off is — fast!"

Skip suited the action to the word with a single swift rip. Harvey's first word was a loud one.

"Ouch!"

With two or three swift slashes Skip cut him loose and turned to Lee.

"Don't rip his tape off that way," said Harvey, rubbing his mouth. "His mouth's cut."

Skip's knife sliced through Lee's bonds, and Lee stood up painfully, stretching and stamping to restore his circulation.

His face set as he braced himself, and then he ripped off his own adhesive.

"Only one way to do it, cut or no cut," he mumbled, pressing his bruised mouth with both hands as the pain made him wince. But then he smiled a crooked smile that trembled with relief, and slapped Skip on the shoulder. "Man! Where did you come from?"

"I came with Harv in the *Fifteen*, and swam underwater from a couple of hundred yards out," Skip explained. "Hey, Harv, how's it going?"

"Okay, so far," said Harv. "If only Gumbo doesn't muff it this time . . ."

"Don't worry. Gumbo won't muff anything that has to do with motors. He'll handle Lee's boat all right."

"*My* boat? Is she over there at the island?"

"Yes."

"Listen, I'm lost," Lee admitted. "What's going on here, anyway? I — hey! Where did you get those?"

He stared at Harvey, who was now wearing a pair of huge, black-rimmed glasses. Harv, in the act of putting a spectacles case back in his pocket, explained hurriedly.

"Always carry an extra pair on outings. Might get broken. Come on, let's get outside and listen. We may have more trouble before we're through."

They hurried outside.

"Can you hear anything, Skip?"

"No. With this onshore breeze, I can't hear my motor any more."

"I hope Gumbo's gotten going by now! He mustn't let them get too close."

"Ssh! Listen!"

They held their breath and strained their ears. Faintly, but unmistakably, they picked up the sound of a motor. Skip whooped.

"That's Lee's boat! That's Gumbo!"

"What is this? What's Gumbo doing in *my* boat?"

"Ssh!"

They listened again.

"And there's the *Fifteen!* I can hear them both now."

"Attaboy, Gumbo! He's making a wide sweep this way, just like I told him to!"

"He's what?" cried Lee. "What's he going to do — lead them right back here?"

"No. He'll twist all over the ocean if he has to."

"But even with the two of them in the *Fifteen,* my boat can't stay out ahead of her forever. They'll catch up with Gumbo —"

"He's got a good head start. Don't worry."

"But why didn't he try to make it to shore? Why —"

Skip interrupted Lee's questions. "Harv! Listen to that!"

Plainly, now, they could hear the *Fifteen's* motor coughing and missing. With a cheer the boys grabbed each other and danced around the beach like lunatics. The coughing continued, and then the motor died.

"Skip! Your calculations were perfect!"

"What are you talking about?" demanded Lee.

"We drained the tank of all but about a cupful of gas!"

"But they have the gravity feed tank, and it's full. I saw Doc lift it out of his way when he got in the boat."

"The line's plugged. And the can's full, all right — full of sea water! I'd love to see their faces when they check it!" Harvey held up his hand. "Listen! Here comes Gumbo!"

For a moment Lee was too flabbergasted to speak. Then he thought of one more detail.

"What about oars, though?"

"They've got oars, all right," nodded Harvey. "We didn't dare take them out, for fear Doc would notice. However, there's one thing they don't have."

"What's that?"

"Oarlocks."

Lee gasped. Then he began to laugh. He had to hold his sides before he was through.

"Do you mean to tell me you've got two vicious criminals sitting out there in open water with no gas and no oarlocks?"

"That was the idea. Of course, they may try to paddle with the oars, though it'll be hard to get anywhere that way with a boat the size of the *Fifteen* in this choppy sea," said Harvey briskly, his mind moving on to final details. "Also, Santos may try to swim ashore here. Either way, they'll probably head for this island, hoping to get to the *Leeway*. So before we leave we'd better make sure she's not in running order."

They ran down onto the wharf. By then Gumbo was nearing the beach. He brought Lee's boat in smartly and leaped ashore with a crow of triumph.

"Hi, guys!"

"Yeay, Gumbo!"

179

He raced over to them.

"Hi, Lee! You all right? Gee, guys, I'm sorry about that alarm clock —"

"Forget it, pal. You finished strong."

While Skip took care of the *Leeway*'s motor, Lee and Harvey searched through the bundles and boxes the men had piled aboard her. They found what they were looking for, far up in the bow.

"Here!" They lifted the steel box up to Gumbo, kneeling on the wharf, and all gathered around it to force the lid open.

Their eyes widened as they peered inside. Lee folded back the thick, waterproof inner lining and lifted out a few of the small green bundles. He riffled one with his thumb.

"One hundred and six grand. Count it for yourself," he said. "Well, this should be all the evidence we need. Let's go."

With Lee and Harvey carrying the precious box between them, they hurried down the beach to Lee's boat.

"My gosh! Are four of us going to pile into this little scow?" snorted Skip.

"One more crack, and only three of us will be going," retorted Lee. "Get aboard. I'm going to have the pleasure of giving you a fine wet ride. Don't worry, we'll make it."

Skip stopped. "Just a minute . . . listen! I think I can hear their voices now."

Once they were all quiet, there was no question about it. The fat man's voice reached them clearly. A frightful string of curses bespattered the night air, the ravings of what was undoubtedly the angriest man they would ever encounter. Harvey shuddered.

180

"We'd better go around the far side of Tree House Island and give them a wide berth. He's got a gun."

They shoved off and settled themselves carefully in the small boat for the slow trip home.

"Well, whatever they do, they can't get far," observed Skip. "They'll still be there when the Coast Guard shows up."

"By then the *Fifteen* may have rocked most of the fight out of them, too," grinned Harv.

"I'll be glad when I get the *Fifteen* back," said Skip. "I hope nothing happens to her."

Gumbo had something on his mind, too.

"I wish we didn't have to tell the part about the alarm clock!" he grumbled.

"Harv," said Lee, "my worst moment on Tree House Island was when Santos climbed up to look in the tree house. All I could do was tell myself that somehow you would manage not to be there by then. But let me ask you one more ques-

181

tion, now. How could you be sure Doc would take the *Fifteen?*"

"Because he's too smart not to think of that angle. I knew he'd think of it — but I figured that nobody, not even a master criminal, would think of a simple thing like checking the gas at a time like that, especially when I left the gas tank where he'd have to move it when he got in. Actually, the whole thing was psychological warfare, from beginning to end," Harvey added in his serious way. Then he laughed. "I guess he decided I was pretty dumb, after all, when I took his word as a gentleman!"

Ahead of them, Tree House Island loomed up out of the dark. As they swung around it they could see the tree house standing out dimly against the sky. Without a word all four turned their heads to look up at it. As the angle changed, the moon's dim rays caused the silver-gray boards to glint faintly for a second or two.

It was an ordinary tree house such as kids had built everywhere for ages past, but it seemed a very special one now. Each of them knew it was one tree house he would never forget as long as he lived.

They put ashore at Toby Henderson's place and telephoned the Coast Guard. An hour later a small flotilla entered Goose Harbor: a Coast Guard cutter with two prisoners aboard; Lee's boat, with Lee and Gumbo in it; and the *Fifteen* with Harvey sitting on the center thwart and Skip once more at the helm.

By that time the whole town had heard the news. It was

182

the first time Goose Harbor had turned out at two o'clock in the morning since the Methodist church burned down thirty years before. By the time the cutter edged alongside the wharf, the waterfront was ablaze with automobile lights. Despite the glare, however, it was soon possible to pick out certain key figures among those waiting in the front rank on the wharf.

"Hey, Skip, look! There's your dad!" cried Harvey.

"Yes, and there's your Aunt Sarah! And there's Uncle Nate!"

Harvey ducked his head and chortled.

"And look who's almost jumping off the wharf. Mr. Eph!"

"And there's Mary beside him. Look at her waving!"

Once Goose Harbor had shaken itself awake at two o'clock in the morning, it knew how to do things up. The welcome for its returning heroes could probably have been heard over in Lanfield.

"Son," said Mr. Ellis, beaming at Skip, "your mother and I —"

"Harvey Harding, I was just worried sick about you young-'uns," announced Aunt Sarah, to nobody's surprise.

Old Mr. Eph glared at Skip and Harvey, harrumphed loudly, and then threw a long arm around each of them and bellowed, "You scoundrels! You young scoundrels, you!" Next he grabbed Lee by the shoulder and whirled a fierce glance around at his granddaughter.

"Well? Here he is! Drat it, girl — don't just stand there!"

"Son," said Mr. Ellis, trying again, "your mother and I are —"

"Clear the way here!" ordered Chief Newton of the local

183

police, bustling importantly. "Got to bring the prisoners ashore."

At the sight of the manacled fat man and Santos, the crowd moved back and fell silent. As Doc stepped onto the wharf, the familiar smile was once again on his face. He paused to glance around, and his small eyes found Harvey. When they did, his portly bow was a masterpiece of murderous implications.

"I can't say it's been a pleasure, lad," he remarked, "but still, I hope we meet again."

"I hope not, Dr. Dillingham," said Harvey, and returned the bow.

Doc glanced over his shoulder at Santos. "Polite. Straightforward," he said. "I like that." And with Santos behind him looking neither to left nor right, the fat man walked on, a bulging figure of evil, smiling to the last.

3 A